A
Christmas Tree
of Stories

SCHOLASTIC
PRESS

Scholastic Children's Books
Commonwealth House, 1–19 New Oxford Street,
London WC1A 1NU
a division of Scholastic Ltd
London ~ New York ~ Toronto ~ Sydney ~ Auckland
Mexico City ~ New Delhi ~ Hong Kong

These stories first published by Scholastic Ltd, 1995, 1997

This anthology copyright © Scholastic Ltd, 1999

ISBN 0 439 01192 2

All rights reserved

Printed and bound in China

10 9 8 7 6 5 4 3 2 1

Acknowledgements

These stories were first published by Scholastic Ltd in *Magical Christmas Stories* and *Wondrous Christmas Stories*.

The following are the copyright owners of the stories:

Mr Mackintosh copyright © 1997 Aileen Paterson

Not Just For Christmas… copyright © 1997 Rob Childs

Dear Santa copyright © 1997 Tessa Krailing

The Umbrella Tree Fairy copyright © 1997 Jean Ure

Sparrow's Special Christmas copyright © 1997 Susan Gates

The Pirates' Christmas Party copyright © 1995 Adèle Geras

The Box of Magic copyright © 1995 Malorie Blackman

Just Like an Angel copyright © 1997 Gillian Cross

Contents

Mr Mackintosh

Aileen Paterson

When Mr Mackintosh came to help out at Lovett's Corner Shop, things were as bad as could be. Mrs Lovett was in hospital and Mr Lovett had gone down with a bad dose of 'flu. The weather had gone wrong too. It hadn't stopped raining for weeks.

It was Andy Lovett who'd suggested putting the notice in the window.

URGENT! TEMPORARY SHOP ASSISTANT REQUIRED FOR XMAS PERIOD. APPLY WITHIN.

"It's no good, Andy," said his dad. "It'll be a miracle if anyone wants a job so near Christmas. I can't pay much anyway."

But Andy wrote it out in his best writing and put

3

it in the window. Somebody had to do something!

Things had been bad enough lately, with Mum in hospital and Dad going round the bend trying to cope on his own. There was no one to help. His London grandma was away in Canada visiting her sister, and his Newcastle grandma had a job. Andy was very fed up. If his mum could see him, she'd give him a hug and say, "Cheer up, gloomyboots! You look like a wet weekend." But Mum wasn't here. It was difficult for his dad to get away from the shop so they could visit her every day. Andy missed her, and he was worried about her and the baby they were waiting for.

Andy missed Mum's cooking too. Dad made fish fingers and beans for tea *every* night. Fish fingers were fine, but not every night.

"They're coming out of my ears," he grumbled to his friend Gideon. "I'll be turning into a fish finger if this goes on."

"Some people might think that was an improvement," laughed his friend.

But now his dad was ill. When he got home from school, he'd found him sitting shivering in their flat at the back of the shop. Andy made him sit by the fire and fetched some aspirins and a cup of tea. Dad wanted to shut the shop, but Andy took his place behind the counter.

That was when he decided to put the notice in the window.

Looking out, he watched the rain pouring down. There was no one about. The rain was filling the gutters, swirling old crisp packets and matchsticks along in its path. Overhead some miserable starlings huddled together on the telephone wires. No one would have dreamt that it was nearly Christmas. The shop didn't look much better. His father seemed to have cancelled Christmas this year. The cards and wrapping paper were lying in a heap in a corner. He hadn't even put their own cards up in the flat.

Suddenly the shop bell began jangling noisily. The door flew open with a loud wharooooshing noise, and a man stepped inside. He stopped halfway to the counter and stood there, looking around him.

Andy looked at the man. He was stocky with rosy cheeks and a pair of old-fashioned wire spectacles on his nose. He was wearing a raincoat and a long blue scarf with white stars all over it. Sandy curls stuck out from under his woolly hat. When he removed his hat off to shake the rain off, Andy noticed that he had a bald spot. One of his curls lay across it, like a piece of crispy bacon on a plate. He wasn't one of their regulars. Andy had never seen him before.

"Can I help you, sir?" asked Andy.

The man smiled.

"Funny, I was just going to ask you the same question! My name is Mackintosh. I've come to enquire about the job advertised in your window. Are you in charge here?"

Andy couldn't believe his ears. The notice had only been in the window for about five minutes, and already someone wanted the job.

"Er … I'm Andy Lovett," he stammered. "It's my dad's shop. He's in the back. Would you like to speak to him?"

The man nodded and followed Andy into the flat to meet Mr Lovett. Andy was dying to stay and see what happened but the shop bell rang again, so he got back to work. Ten minutes and three customers later, his father appeared with their visitor. They shook hands. Mr Mackintosh put on his woolly hat again and headed for the door.

"Cheerio!" he cried, waving to Andy. "See you both in the morning."

Then he was gone.

"Well, Andy," said his father. "You can take your advert out of the window. It did the trick. Mr Mackintosh is going to help us out till Christmas Eve. He seems a nice sort of chap. Used to have a little shop like ours up in Edinburgh. Let's hope he soon gets the hang of things here. Now, son, if you don't mind, I'm going to lock up and go to bed. I feel terrible. Can you make your own supper tonight? There's loads of fish fingers in the freezer."

"I know," said Andy.

In the morning his dad's 'flu was worse. Andy made him stay in bed then he telephoned for the doctor to come later. He was busy trying to eat some toast and bring in the milk crates and news-papers, when Mr Mackintosh arrived, and took over. Andy gave a sigh of relief. It was time to leave for school, and he could see Gideon waiting for him at the corner.

"Off you go, laddie," said Mr Mackintosh. "I'll take good care of your dad and the shop, I promise."

"Thanks," said Andy. "Bye, Dad."

It was only when he was halfway to school that he noticed that it wasn't raining. The sun had come out at last.

After school, Andy and Gideon walked home together. Gideon told him about his dad's new taxi, and about his granny. She had flown all the way from Jamaica to spend Christmas with them. He said she was a bit disappointed that there was no snow in London. She'd never seen snow. Andy said he wasn't sure there would be a proper Christmas in his house, with one thing and another.

When they reached the shop, Gideon said he'd see Andy in the morning, and headed home. Andy pushed open the shop door. He just stood and stared when he got inside. The floor was gleaming, the shelves had been dusted and tidied. The window was full of sweets and chocolates, and someone had painted snowflakes on the glass. There were red and gold Christmas decorations on the walls, and silver stars hanging from the ceiling. It was beautiful! And there was music playing. Not the music they had in the supermarket that his dad called tosh. No. This was like a faraway choir singing carols from long ago. *At last* Andy felt the tingle inside that comes when Christmas time is almost here.

Mr Mackintosh, dressed in a rainbow-striped jumper, was busy serving a queue of customers.

"Can I give you a hand?" asked Andy.

"Hello, Andy," said Mr Mackintosh. "I'm fine, thank you. I'm enjoying myself! Pop in and see your dad. He'll be pleased to see you."

"Righto. The shop looks great!"

The flat looked nice too. Their Christmas cards were hanging above the fireplace. A wonderful smell of cooking was coming from the kitchen. His dad was tucked up in bed reading. He looked much better.

"Hello," he said. "How was school?"

"Not bad. Quite good actually. We had a concert this afternoon. The headmaster did magic tricks, and Miss Miller did a tapdance!"

His dad smiled.

"Did the doctor come?"

"Yes. He said I was to stay in bed for a couple of days. Good job we have Mr Mackintosh to help. I phoned your mum to say we wouldn't be in to see her till I'm better. She's feeling fine, and she sends you her love."

Things were looking up, thought Andy. He felt happier than he had been for ages. Ever since Mr Mackintosh had arrived *everything* was better.

After the shop closed, it was time for supper. It was a lot better than usual too. Mr Mackintosh was a good cook. He said he had never heard of fish fingers. He didn't know fish had any! Instead they all had chicken stew and baked potatoes, and apple crumble to follow. It was delicious.

Mr Mackintosh was full of surprises!

There were more next day.

"I've got a job for you," said Mr Mackintosh

when Andy got home. There, in the sitting-room, stood a Christmas tree in a red tub.

"It's just a wee present from me. Christmas isn't Christmas without a tree," he said, handing Andy a box of ornaments and lights.

"I'm sure you'll manage to make it look bonny, and we can put all your parcels underneath."

"PARCELS?" said Andy.

"Yes. Parcels. Didn't I mention it? The postman's delivered a big pile of them for you all."

Andy enjoyed decorating the tree all by himself. Besides the ornaments and fairy lights, there were little toys and chocolate teddy bears. He tied them all carefully on to the branches, then last of all there was a big glittering star for the top. Mr Mackintosh came in from the shop with loads of gaily wrapped parcels, and they put them all around the tree. Last of all, Andy switched off the light in the room and Mr Mackintosh switched on the tree lights… Andy's dad came through in his dressing-gown to watch. It was the twinkliest, best Christmas tree any of them had ever seen!

The day after that was *full* of good things. It was

the last day of school before the holidays, and each class had a party. When the school bell rang, Andy and Gideon raced out of the gates, and there, parked outside, was Gideon's dad's taxi.

"Special orders from Mr Mackintosh!" said Gideon's dad. When they arrived at the shop, Andy's dad was waiting for him. He was better at last. He was even dressed in his coat and scarf.

"Let's go, Andy," he said. "Your mum phoned. The baby is on its way!"

Gideon and Mr Mackintosh waved to them till the taxi disappeared.

It was late when they got back. Mr Mackintosh put their supper in the oven and waited for them. At last the flat door flew open.

"It's a *boy*!" cried Andy and his dad. "And they're both fine."

"Tell me all about it."

"He's got a loud voice," laughed Andy. "And he's got red hair like me, and he's strong. He wouldn't let my finger go!" His eyes were shining with happiness.

12

"He sounds just terrific," said Mr Mackintosh. "I like new babies. They look just like a dumpling in a hankie. Has he got a name yet?"

"Mum says we're to call him after you, for coming to help us at Christmas. What's your name?"

Mr Mackintosh went very red, and blew his nose. "That's the nicest Christmas present I've ever had. My name is Noel."

"Then our baby is Noel Lovett!" said Andy and his dad.

On Christmas Eve it was time for Mr Mackintosh to go. He had done his job and now it was over. He said goodbye to all the Lovett family. Mrs Lovett was home again with the baby. Mr Mackintosh had put presents for everyone under the tree, and Andy handed him his present.

"Thank you for everything, from all of us. Please come back and see us again. We're going to miss you."

"I'll do my best," smiled Mr Mackintosh. "Merry Christmas, Andy."

He waved goodbye to them all and walked up the

street. There were snowflakes drifting in the wind. Mr Mackintosh caught one in his hand. Gideon's granny won't be disappointed, he thought. He thought of them all waking up tomorrow to a white Christmas. He thought of the new baby. "That's what Christmas is all about," he said to himself.

He climbed to the top of the hill and looked back at Lovett's Corner Shop. Everything had gone well. If it hadn't been for Andy, he would never have had the chance to come and help. He put his hand in his raincoat pocket and took out the present Andy had given him. When he unwrapped it, he laughed. It was a harmonica! He put it in his mouth and began to play. The snow swirled round him as his hat and scarf and raincoat dissolved and changed into a long gown of shimmering white. His wings unfolded and lifted in the night wind. Mr Mackintosh, still playing, rose into the air and flew up through the snowclouds into the blue sky of Heaven.

Not Just For
Christmas...

Rob Childs

J ames woke up very early with an extra special sense of excitement.

"Christmas Day!" He felt like shouting it out. He had been looking forward to this day for so long, and now – at last – it was here!

Trembling, James sat up in bed and rubbed his eyes. He opened them again, slowly, but everywhere was dark and he still couldn't see anything.

He tried not to be too disappointed. "Maybe they're with all my other presents," he murmured. "Santa must have been by now."

James liked to talk to himself, to hear the sound of his voice in the darkness. He was glad he had his own bedroom. It was his private little world, a place where he knew that nobody else would be nearby to listen. Like Hannah, for instance.

His sister was OK to play with at times, he

admitted, but she was only five, three years younger than him. Her never-ending chatter often irritated him, especially if she got too big for her boots and tried to do things for him.

"I wonder where everything will be this year?" he said aloud.

It was part of the family fun at Christmas. After Santa's visit, Mum and Dad would hide the presents all over the house and then go back to sleep. He and Hannah had to wait, bursting with anticipation, until their parents said they could start looking. James considered whether he might risk going to wake them up yet so he could begin the hunt.

"Bet it's still a bit too early."

He reached under the pillows instead for his favourite toy soldier, but his fingers first touched a piece of paper. It was a copy of his letter to Santa, put there for safe keeping, and he gave it a superstitious pat.

Then his hand closed around the small plastic figure with a gun and he whipped it out with a flourish. "Bang!" he cried, pretending to shoot at

18

the one-eared teddy bear that lay by his side. "Bang! Bang!"

He chuckled as Teddy had to dive down on to the carpet to escape the bullets. James leapt out of bed after him and the fight went on as Sam the soldier chased Teddy across the floor.

"Oooh! It's too cold!" James said, with a shiver. He grabbed Teddy and scrambled back under the duvet, wriggling right down until he was completely covered. Snuggling up with Teddy, he felt warm again and happy, hoping it wouldn't be long before he'd be able to see all the pretty lights on the Christmas tree. He closed his eyes and crossed his fingers.

"James! James! Wake up!"

He was being pushed and pulled about, but he stayed underneath the thick duvet out of sight.

"I *am* awake," came his muffled voice. "Go away!"

"You were fast asleep," Hannah insisted. "I was awake before you."

His tousled head shot out from the covers. "No, you weren't. I've been awake for years."

"No, you haven't! I was up first this morning."

"Rubbish! I even helped Santa empty his sack!"

Hannah gave up. She could never win such silly arguments with her stubborn big brother.

"It's time!" she announced instead.

James knew exactly what she meant. "I know," he replied. "I was just waiting for you, that's all, so we went in together."

She gave him a funny look, but knew that all the faces she might pull were just wasted on James. "Come on, then. Let's go in!"

Tingling with excitement, the children crept along the landing and pushed open the door to their parents' bedroom.

"Dad's snoring," James hissed.

"Goodie!" giggled Hannah. "We can both sneak up on him and make him jump!"

James felt his sister's hand slide into his as they tiptoed into the room towards Dad's side of the bed.

"Oh no, you don't, you two!" came a voice in the darkness. "I know what you're up to!"

"Mummy!" Hannah squealed. "Oh, you spoiled it!"

Mum laughed. "You little pests. Do you know what time it is?"

"No," said James, "but I do know what day it is. It's Christmas Day!"

"Come on in," Mum invited them, drawing back the duvet covers. "Come and have a Christmas cuddle."

Hannah slithered in first for a kiss from Mum, quickly followed by James. Dad rolled over. "Who's the elephant with cold feet?" he grumbled sleepily.

"James, Daddy!" Hannah cried. "Happy Christmas!"

"Christmas is cancelled!"

"No, it's not!" they chorused.

"Yes, it is," he said. "Haven't you heard? Santa's gone on holiday!"

"No, he hasn't. You're just teasing," James chuckled, punching Dad on the shoulder. "He only goes on holiday after he's delivered all our presents. It's time now."

"It's time, Mummy," echoed Hannah. "It's time!"

"I can see we're not going to get any peace," Mum said. "OK, it's time. Off you go while I make a drink."

The children whooped their delight and shot out of the bed, desperate to be the one to find the first present. They always knew whose it was by the wrapping. Hannah's gifts had ribbon around them and a bow, while James's were tied up loosely with string. He loved pulling off the string and tearing open the packaging to see what was inside.

"Found one straight away!" he screamed proudly as he squirmed underneath the bed. "And it's mine!"

He ripped the string and wrapping paper away from the box and held it up to his nose. "Hmm, yummy smell! My favourite chocs!"

His next discovery, at the bottom of a wardrobe, didn't have anything round it at all. It didn't need it. James knew what it was as soon as he felt around the shoes and touched it. "Wow! A football. Thanks!"

Dad laughed. "Santa would have had a terrible job trying to wrap up a football! He obviously didn't bother."

James stopped searching for anything else for a while, dribbling the ball around the bedroom with his bare feet and knocking into things as he lost control.

"Hey! Steady on, superstar," cried Dad, getting out of bed himself at last. "You'll go and break something and then we'll all be in trouble. Let's wait till we get outside in the garden later."

Shrieks and squeals from Hannah confirmed her own successes, and the children spent a very happy hour up and down the stairs, poking and probing into cupboards and drawers. James even found a tape of one of his best-loved stories lying in the bath.

"Good job I didn't turn the taps on first," he grinned.

Mum laughed. "No danger of you volunteering to have a bath, is there, you mucky pup."

She caught Dad's eye and they smiled at what she had just said. Mum put down her cup of tea and pulled the two children gently towards her on the sofa.

"Uncle John is coming round later this morning," she said, giving them both a hug. "He's bringing along something else for you, although it's not really a Christmas present. It's something even more special."

Hannah's eyes widened. "Is it a pony?" she gasped.

Mum shook her head and smiled. "No guessing allowed. We want it to be a surprise."

Mum supervised their washing and dressing while Dad prepared some breakfast. "What time is Uncle John coming?" asked Hannah the moment she trotted into the kitchen.

"Soon," Dad said. "You'll have to be patient and play with all your new toys until he gets here."

"Will we be able to play with what he's bringing?" she persisted.

"Still trying to work out what it can be, aren't you?" he laughed. "But yes, you'll certainly be able to play with it."

James was strangely quiet at the table, nibbling at a piece of toast, and Dad attempted to cheer him up. "How about us two going out to kick your new ball about a bit, eh?"

James nodded, but didn't look up. "Have I found *all* my presents yet?" he asked instead.

"Not quite," Mum replied. "I think there are still a couple of things hidden away."

"I'll help him look for them," Hannah piped up.

"No you won't!" cried James. "I don't need any help. I'll find them when I'm ready."

Hannah was about to answer him back until Mum shot her a warning glance and she swiftly changed the subject. "This is the best Christmas ever," she beamed. "I've got everything I wanted. Have you, James?"

"Not yet," he said simply and slid away from the table to play with the toy cars that he'd left near the fire.

When the bell rang, the children rushed to the door, both wanting to be the one to open it. Hannah won the race – as usual.

"Hi, kids!" Uncle John greeted them. "Merry Christmas, everyone!"

Hannah looked all around for whatever it was that Uncle John was supposed to have with him. There was nothing to be seen.

"Did you like my presents I got Santa to leave for you?" he asked and then laughed at their blank expressions. "Just like me when I was your age. Too busy opening the boxes to bother with the labels!"

"Uncle John bought you those horrible noisy, electronic games," Dad explained, slipping his younger brother a wink. "Typical! He won't be the one who's got to put up with all the din every time you play with them."

"Oh, thank you, Uncle John!" Hannah said politely as he picked her up to give her a peck on the cheek.

"Thanks, I'll have some fun with that, annoying Dad," grinned James.

Uncle John acted as though he'd just remembered something. "Oh, yes, I almost forgot. There's another thing you'll have a lot of fun with, too. I've left it in the car."

Still carrying Hannah, he led the way out on to the drive, and his niece suddenly let out a shriek. From her high vantage point, she could see into the back of his estate car. "A puppy! A real puppy!"

She squirmed out of his grasp and ran to the car to stare through the rear window. "Oh, it's beautiful. It's so cute. What big eyes!"

"It's a *she*," Uncle John said. "And she's not so cute when she leaves little puddles all over your carpet and inside your car!"

The children laughed and demanded the car be open so that they could hold the puppy.

"Thanks for looking after her for a couple of days, John," Mum said. "Hope she hasn't been too much trouble to you."

"None at all," he grinned. "Apart from the puddles!"

"What is she?" asked James.

"A labrador," said Dad. "And she's just seven weeks old."

James stroked the puppy's short, stubby nose and chin as Hannah cuddled her. "What shall we call her?" he wondered.

"Actually, she's already got a name," said Mum. "It's Misty."

"Who gave her that?"

"The people at the kennels where she was born."

James considered it for a moment. "OK, Misty's a fine name."

Mum smiled with relief. "Do you like her?" she

asked anxiously.

He nodded. "I've often wanted a dog to play with."

"I know, but we weren't quite sure if it would be a good thing," Dad said. "Especially after that big dog down the street knocked you over."

"It wasn't the dog's fault," James said. "I must have stepped on its tail or something and hurt it."

"You cried," gloated his sister. "I remember you crying."

"So?" he demanded. "You would have done too. You're always crying. It just made me jump, that's all. I didn't know what was happening."

"Anyway, never mind now, don't argue," Mum said, prising the puppy out of Hannah's arms. "Let James hold Misty for a while, darling."

Hannah looked down at her dress in dismay. "Oh! I'm all wet!"

Everyone laughed. "Serves you right for squeezing her so tight," Dad chuckled.

"Let's take Misty into the back garden and play ball," said James as Mum led Hannah into the house to change her clothes.

Sma...
11/12/20...
Borrowed: 8
Overdue: 0
Reservations: 0
Ready for collection...

Items that you already...

Title: Itchy, scritchy, scitc...
ID: 54300000927284
Due: 03 January 2020

Title: Little Fish and mu...
ID: 54300000994250
Due: 03 January 2020

Title: Little unicorn's Chr...
54300005116503
...January 2020

...age for Santa
...00348080

Title: Pr... 2020
ID: 54300...
Due: 03 January 2020

Title: They came from Planet batooloo!
ID: 44139001453053
Due: 03 January 2020

Title: Vehicles
ID: 54300005054928
Due: 03 January 2020

Thank you for visiting Great Hollands
Library.

Please keep this receipt safe.

Contact us:

Tel: 01344 424095

Email: GreatHollands.Library@bracknell-
forest.gov.uk

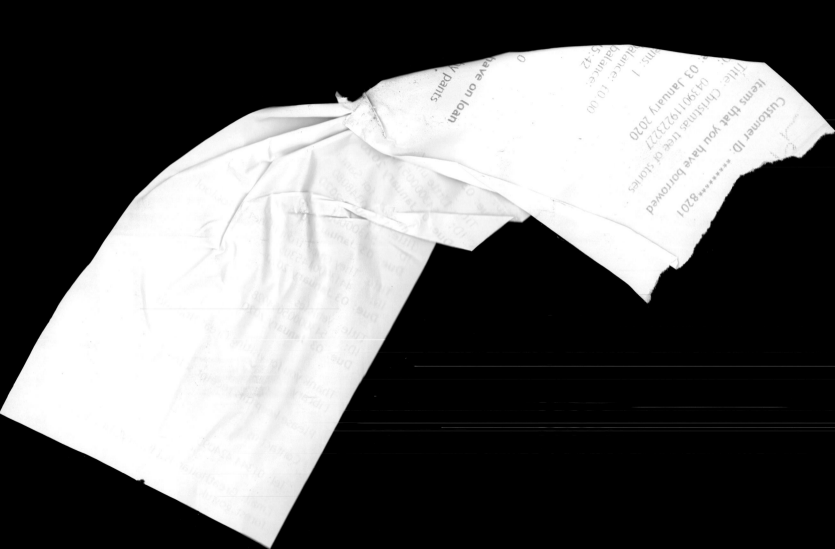

Customer ID: ********8201

Items that you have borrowed

Title: Christmas tree of stories
04190119232227
Due: 03 January 2020

Total items: 1
Balance: £5.42

Items that you have on loan
0

His new football was far too big for the puppy and James kicked a small ball across the lawn instead. It was ideal. The ball made a rattling sound as it rolled along, attracting her attention, and Misty scampered after it with yelps of excitement.

Dad and Uncle John joined in the game, laughing at the puppy's antics. The ball was just the right size for Misty and light enough for her to nose it through the grass in a wayward dribble. Dad passed the rattling ball to James who timed his next kick perfectly, sending it flying into the bushes by the fence.

"Goal!" cried Uncle John. "Great stuff, James. We'll have you playing for United yet."

"Rovers!" James corrected him. "They're the best team in the land."

The puppy soon grew weary. She squatted on the lawn and then settled down for a nap.

"Dog-tired! Just like the Rovers' players," joked Uncle John to tease James again about his favourite football team.

Dad carried Misty inside for a drink of water from the shiny metal bowl that his brother had also brought with him. She lapped noisily at the water, spilling most of it on to the kitchen floor.

"Looks like we'll get through a lot of newspapers, soaking up all her messes," Mum chuckled. "I just hope Misty realizes what a lucky puppy she is, coming to live with us until she grows up."

"Till she grows up?" repeated James in alarm. "What do you mean?"

Mum put her arm around his shoulders and led him through to the lounge, calling Hannah to join them. As the family sat together near the Christmas tree, Misty curled up asleep on the rug in front of the fire.

"Misty doesn't know it yet," Mum said, "but when she's older and specially trained, she's going to have a very important job to do."

"What's that?" James interrupted impatiently, but the answer stunned him into silence.

"She will become a guide dog for a blind person."

Dad picked up the story. "But while she's a puppy, she needs to be looked after and loved just like any normal pet. That's where we come in. We've decided to be puppy-walkers."

"Puppy-walkers!" giggled Hannah. "What a funny name!"

"Perhaps it is," Mum smiled, "because we'll be doing far more than just walking Misty. She'll be one of the family for a whole year."

"But then has she got to go to somebody else?" asked James.

"I'm afraid so," Dad answered. "But we can always take on another puppy after that, if we want to."

"We thought it might be better this way at first," Mum explained. "Just to let you get used to having a dog around the house. See how you get on together."

"We'll get on just fine," he said seriously. "I've never heard of people being puppy-walkers. It's a good idea."

James lay down next to the puppy on the rug, stroking her soft fur and gently fondling her large, floppy ears. He was rewarded with little grunts of contentment, almost like purring, and then felt his hand being licked by a rasping, wet tongue.

"Ooh! It tickles!" he chuckled.

Hannah didn't intend to be left out. She wanted to be licked too, and Misty rolled her tongue along the girl's bare arm as far as she could reach, sending Hannah into fits of giggles.

"Misty certainly won't be going short of love and fuss here, I can see that," Uncle John laughed. "She's fallen on her feet all right – and she knows it!"

As the puppy dozed, Hannah disappeared to try on her new ballet costume, but James stayed at Misty's side, his hand resting on one of her stretched out legs. "She feels so warm," he murmured happily.

"You look wonderful together, lying there," Mum told him. "We'll have to take a photo of you both like that."

There was no chance now. Misty was awake again – and looking for a spot of mischief. She found a willing partner in James, equally eager to play and tumble about.

"Here you are," said Dad. "Have one of my old socks to play tug-of-war with. Dogs love that game."

"Hope it's a clean one and not too smelly," laughed James, who soon felt a determined tugging at the other end of the sock.

"Misty doesn't seem to mind, anyway," Dad grinned.

James let Misty win some of the battles, but she always brought the sock straight back, nudging him to grab hold of it again. Then he decided to throw it away for her to fetch.

The sock landed right on top of the Christmas cake on the table.

"Good job your mum didn't see that!" cried Uncle John, lifting it off quickly and returning it to James. "Try again."

He did, and this time it went into the trifle!

"I think you're better at kicking than throwing," said Uncle John.

The sock came back with a little trace of cream which Misty soon found. She licked her lips with pleasure at the taste.

James played with Misty almost all day in between her frequent snoozes and feeding times. He even forgot to search for his remaining presents until just before bedtime. He wanted Misty to sleep in his bedroom with him as well, but Mum had to be very firm about that.

"She's better off in the kitchen," Mum said. "She needs a place of her own at night too, just like you. And I can put plenty of newspaper all over the floor there around her dog basket!"

Mum sat on the side of his bed and read him a story. "Have you enjoyed having a puppy to play with?" she asked, before saying good night.

James nodded several times. "We're going to have great fun, Misty and me, while she's with us. I can teach her lots of things."

"Yes, like how to get into all sorts of trouble, no doubt," Mum laughed. "And how to get all mucky!"

"Can I have a dog of my own one day?"

"Of course. When you're older. You'll be able to go everywhere together then."

James grinned. "I'll call mine Sam."

"Why Sam?"

James shrugged, unwilling to admit to his soldier's name. "I just like the sound of it."

Mum bent over to kiss him and caught sight of a

piece of paper sticking out from underneath his pillow. She guessed what it was. James had insisted on having a copy of the letter she'd written to Santa for him. Mum remembered off by heart the words that he'd wanted her to write, but she couldn't resist the temptation to read them again now.

Mum quietly slid the paper away from the pillow without James realizing what she was doing. He lay with a happy, peaceful expression on his face, his eyes closed.

A few silent tears escaped from hers as she read over the short letter:

Dear Santa,

I hope you are well. My name is James and I am eight years old. Please can I have a new pair of eyes at Christmas? I keep bumping into things. I know this will be difficult, but I'm sure you will find a way of doing it somehow.

Thank you very much.

Love James

P.S. It would even be nice to see my pesky little sister as well.

*   *   *

Mum slipped the paper back into place and kissed James again. That lovely picture of him lying cosily beside Misty in the glow of the fire swam into her mind. "I'm so glad you like your new pair of eyes, my darling," she whispered.

He smiled and his eyes flickered open, staring up at her blindly.

Author's note:

The Guide Dogs for the Blind Association run puppy-walking schemes in many parts of the country. Families take a puppy, usually a labrador or a golden retriever, into their home to rear as an ordinary pet for the first year of its life. The young dog then goes to stay at a special training centre to learn how to become a guide dog, but a blind person needs to be at least sixteen before they can own one.

Dear Santa

Tessa Krailing

Thomas was halfway through a slice of pizza when Dad dropped his bombshell. "By the way, kids," he said casually, "we shan't be spending Christmas at home this year. We're going up north to spend it with Grandad."

Thomas stopped eating and stared at him with his mouth open.

"Oh, brilliant!" said Kerry, his older sister. "Will there be snow?"

"Almost certainly," said Mum. "Thomas, please close your mouth. A half-chewed piece of pizza is not a pretty sight."

Thomas finished chewing and swallowed hastily. "But – but we can't," he stammered. "We can't go away at Christmas."

"Why not?" asked Dad.

Thomas went red. "Because – because we never

go away at Christmas. We always spend it at home."

"Oh, don't be such a stick-in-the-mud," said Kerry. "It'll be fun at Grandad's. You were only a baby last time we visited him so you don't remember what it's like. We'll be able to build a snowman and go sledging and all that sort of stuff."

"Besides," said Mum, "the poor old man will be on his own this year, so it's only right we should go and keep him company. Nobody should be left alone at Christmas."

"But why can't he come down south to us?" asked Thomas.

"Because he has to stay and look after the animals," said Dad. "It gets very cold up north in December. He can't possibly leave the herd at this time of year."

Thomas pushed his plate away. Suddenly he couldn't eat any more.

Mum gave him a curious look. "What's the problem, Thomas? Why don't you want to spend Christmas with Grandad?"

"I'd rather stay at home," Thomas mumbled.

"Well, you can if you like," said Dad. "But it'll be pretty miserable here on your own. No Christmas dinner…"

"No tree," said Mum.

"And no presents!" said Kerry with a grin.

Thomas went even redder. He pushed back his chair and ran upstairs to his room and threw himself on the bed.

What on earth was he going to do?

A week ago he had sent a letter to Santa asking for certain things he would like for Christmas. Well, one certain thing in particular – a pair of rollerblades. His eyes misted over, just thinking about them. He didn't care about anything else. He wouldn't even mind if he had only one present this Christmas, as long as it was a pair of roller-blades. He'd shown Mum the letter before he sent it and she said she thought there was a fair chance he might be lucky.

But if they went to stay with Grandad for Christmas, *how would Santa know where to deliver their presents?*

No one else seemed troubled about it. They

obviously hadn't realized this could be a major problem. It wasn't that he didn't want to stay with Grandad. He loved Grandad. At any other time of year he would be only too happy to go up north and keep him company.

But he didn't want to be away from home at Christmas.

Thomas knelt on the bed to study the racing car calendar over his bed. Today was 10 December. What if he wrote another letter, telling Santa about the change of plan? Would it reach him in time?

He took out his writing pad and wrote a note in his best and clearest handwriting:

DEAR SANTA,
WE SHAN'T BE HOME THIS CHRISTMAS. WE ARE GOING UP NORTH TO STAY WITH GRANDAD.
LOVE, THOMAS
PS: IT WAS ROLLERBLADES.

Just as he finished the envelope there came a

knock at the door. Hastily he folded the piece of paper and stuffed it inside.

Mum's head appeared round the door. "It's only me," she said. "Thomas, are you feeling all right?"

"Yeah, fine," he assured her. And it was true, he felt a lot better now.

"Only you seemed a bit upset downstairs. You don't really mind going to stay with Grandad, do you?"

"No, I don't mind." He covered the envelope with his hand.

"What have you got there?" Mum asked.

"Er – just a letter."

"You've written a letter?" She looked astonished. "Who to?"

"Um, well, er—" He decided to tell the truth. "I thought I'd better let Santa know we'll be at Grandad's for Christmas. Otherwise ... well, he might deliver our presents to the wrong address."

"Oh, I see. How sensible of you." She gave him a teasing look. "Is that why you didn't want to go away?"

"Well ... yes, I suppose it was."

"Oh, Thomas! Why didn't you say so?"

"I was afraid you'd think I was stupid."

"Of course I wouldn't. Here, give me the letter." She held out her hand. "I'll post it for you."

"Thanks." He gave it to her.

No sooner had she left the room than Thomas remembered it had no stamp. Would she notice? He'd better make sure. He ran down the stairs after her, but when he reached the door of the living-room he heard voices and stopped.

"…written this letter," Mum was saying. "He was afraid that Santa wouldn't know where he'd gone."

Dad chuckled softly. "Poor Thomas. Do you think we should tell him yet?"

"No, he's still very young. Let's leave it a while longer."

Thomas felt deeply hurt. Mum had promised she wouldn't think he was being stupid and now she was laughing about him with Dad. And what was it they didn't think they should tell him yet? He hated secrets – unless of course he was the person keeping them. Did Kerry know? His whole family seemed to be ganging up on him.

44

Fed up, he turned round and stomped back upstairs. Some rotten Christmas this was going to be, stuck in the frozen North with no presents!

On Christmas Eve they packed everything into the car and set off for Grandad's. The journey on the motorway took hours. Hours and hours and hours. And all the while it was getting colder. Colder and colder and colder. When they got out of the car at a service station their breath froze on the air. "Anyone fancy some hot soup?" asked Mum taking out a Thermos.

"OK, but we mustn't stop long," said Dad. "We've still a long way to go."

They drank chicken soup out of mugs and set off again. This time Mum did the driving. She and Dad had agreed to take it in turns because it was such a long journey.

Soon Thomas fell asleep, resting his head against Kerry's shoulder. In his dreams he saw his home, dark and shuttered and empty, and Santa peering down the chimney.

"Well, here's a rum thing," Santa muttered under

his breath. "No one at home. I'll have to give their presents to someone else. Ah well, I daresay some young boy or girl will be delighted to receive these rollerblades…"

Thomas awoke with a start. "No!" he shouted. "No, don't do that!"

"Don't do what?" asked Kerry. "I haven't moved for the last half hour. Could you sit up, please? I've got cramp in my arm."

Then he realized that he was still in the car. Still travelling north. Still on the way to Grandad's.

And it was still Christmas Eve.

He peered out of the window and saw they were no longer on the motorway but travelling along a straight, narrow road lined with fir trees. "Where are we?" he asked. "Are we nearly there?"

"Not yet," said Dad from the driving seat. He and Mum must have changed over while Thomas was asleep.

On and on they sped. Soon the countryside began to look different, more rugged and hilly, with fast moving rivers. Thomas began to feel drowsy again. He drifted in and out of sleep, only half aware of arriving at a port ... and driving on to a ferry ... and driving off again. Next time he woke up properly they were crossing a narrow bridge over a ravine.

"Oh, good," said Kerry. "It's starting to snow."

Large white flakes fluttered down from the sky and burst against the windscreen. Before long, Dad had to switch the wipers on. Soon he could hardly see where he was going. He slowed his speed right down, peering through a lacy curtain of ice at the fast-disappearing track.

"I hope we make it before dark," Mum said anxiously. "It would be awful if we had to spend Christmas huddled inside the car."

"Oh, we'll make it," said Dad, trying to sound confident. "It's not much further. It can't be."

"I'm hungry," complained Kerry.

Thomas didn't say anything. Miserably he stared through the car window at the wintry scene outside, wishing he was at home by the fire.

Then, just when he had given up hope of ever arriving anywhere, Dad said, "There it is! Look, on our left. I can see a light in the window."

"Oh, thank goodness!" Mum sounded ready to cry with relief.

At that moment the car skidded sideways and came to a stop. Dad tried to get it started again, but it refused to budge. He got out to investigate.

"We've run into a snowdrift," he reported. "You'd better get out. We'll have to walk the last bit."

It was freezing outside. Through deep snow they made their way towards Grandad's house, past the barn where the animals were kept, past the garage and the outhouses. By the time they reached the front door Thomas's jeans were soaked, his feet felt like blocks of ice and his hands were numb.

Then, suddenly, the door opened and Grandad stood there, beaming all over his red, cheerful face.

"At last!" he exclaimed. "I was beginning to worry about you. Come in, come in!"

They trooped inside. Grandad hugged them one by one, scratching their cheeks with his bushy white beard.

"My, how you've grown!" he remarked when it was Thomas's turn. "Yet it can't be more than a year since I came down south to visit you."

"Eighteen months," said Mum, taking off her coat. "And far too long since we last came north. I must say you've made it look very cosy and welcoming."

Grandad beamed at her. "I'm glad you think so."

The house was old, with thick stone walls and dark beams, but Grandad had strung up tinselly decorations and coloured lights. Festoons of cards hung from the rafters and in one corner stood a huge Christmas tree, reaching almost to the ceiling. Thomas began to feel more cheerful.

Until Dad remarked, "I see you've made some alterations. That gas fire's new, isn't it."

Grandad nodded. "New this year. So much more convenient than having to fetch coal in from outside."

Oh, no! Thomas stared in horror at the large, modern gas fire with its pretend flames flickering around pretend coals. It completely filled the fireplace, leaving no gaps anywhere.

How on earth could Santa deliver their presents if the chimney was blocked up?

He couldn't think of anything else all evening. During supper he kept imagining Santa trying to get through and finding himself stuck behind the gas fire. What would he do? Would he give up in disgust – or, worse, would he be trapped there for ever and ever?

"This stew is wonderful, Grandad," said Kerry. "It's warming me right through."

"That's good," he said. "Thomas, you're very quiet. Don't you like it?"

Startled, Thomas looked up. "Like what?"

"The stew, dimwit!" said Kerry.

"He's tired out after the journey," Mum said quickly. "I think he should go to bed pretty soon."

For once Thomas didn't argue.

"I've put you in the attic," Grandad explained as he took him upstairs. "The bed's a bit narrow but it should be comfortable as long as you don't try to move about too much." He opened the door and switched on the light. "There. Think you can manage?"

"Yes, thanks," said Thomas.

Grandad smiled at him kindly. "It's very good of

you to come all this way to see me. I expect you'd far rather have stayed at home for Christmas."

Thomas was tempted to tell the truth, but he didn't want to hurt Grandad's feelings. "No, it's OK," he said gruffly. "I expect I'll enjoy it when I'm not so tired."

"Good boy." Grandad patted his shoulder. "Give me a yell if you need anything." He closed the door and left.

When Thomas had washed and undressed he went to look out of the window. At last it had stopped snowing. A brilliant moon lit up the scene, casting blue shadows over the frozen countryside. Below him lay a large white square of snow with not a mark on it, not even a footprint. It looked like a blank sheet of paper...

Suddenly he had a brilliant idea!

He pulled on his dressing-gown and crept downstairs, past the living-room where everyone was talking and laughing, until he came to the boots he was wearing when he arrived. He pulled them on, quietly opened the front door and stepped outside.

It didn't seem so cold now that it had stopped

snowing. Everywhere was silent, except for slight sounds of movement in the barn where the animals were kept. His boots made a scrunching noise in the snow, leaving a deep imprint. As soon as he reached the large white square he began to tread with care, turning and twisting as he spelt out the message with his footprints:

DEAR SANTA
DON'T TRY TO COME DOWN THE CHIMNEY
LOVE, THOMAS

When he had finished he stood still and read over what he had written. To be honest, it looked a bit of a mess from down here, just a lot of downtrodden snow, but from above the message should be easy to read. At least it would save poor Santa getting stuck behind the gas fire – and with luck he might find somewhere else to leave their presents.

Thomas walked back to the front door. He opened it quietly and stepped into the hall. As he took off his boots he heard the others still talking in the living-room.

"…so he actually wrote a letter to Santa!" That was Dad's voice, shaking with laughter.

"And I offered to post it for him!" said Mum.

Thomas went hot all over. So they still thought he was a big joke, just because he'd tried to let Santa know where he'd be spending Christmas. Well, if they looked outside the front door they'd probably laugh even louder.

Then Kerry said, "I think we should tell him. Don't you, Grandad?"

"No need," said Grandad. "He'll find out for himself when the time is right."

Now they were talking about the secret again. It must be something they all knew about, even Grandad. This time Thomas felt more angry than hurt. He was on the point of bursting into the room and demanding to know what it was when he heard Grandad say, "Well, it's time I went and did my duty. The animals will be getting restless."

"You'd better wrap up well," said Mum. "It's very cold out there."

"Don't worry, my old fleecy coat keeps me warm as toast."

The living-room door started to open. Guiltily Thomas shot up the stairs just as Grandad came out into the hall. He went back into the attic bedroom and looked out of the window.

Oh, no! Even seen from above, the words were very difficult to read. His footprints seemed to wander all over the place and the letters weren't at all clear. It was hard to tell the 'D's from the 'O's, the 'M's looked more like 'W's and the 'E's and 'S's like figure 8's. In fact the message appeared to say:

O8AR 8ANTA
  OONT TRY TD CDW8 OOWN TH8 CHIWN8Y
  LDV8, THDWA8

And then there was a long, wavering line where he had made his way back to the front door. Thomas groaned. Santa would *never* be able to read it, not even if he was looking down at it from above.

At that moment the front door opened and

Grandad appeared below, dressed in a bulky coat with a hood. He set off towards the barn without even glancing at the churned-up snow in front of the house.

The animals seemed to hear him coming. They stamped their feet as he approached and Thomas heard a faint jingling sound, as if they were wearing some kind of harness. Grandad opened the barn door and went inside.

A few minutes later he reappeared, leading a line of deer. At least, Thomas supposed they must be deer because they had antlers. In fact they looked more like – yes, how strange, they looked more like reindeer. But of course that was impossible. If Grandad kept reindeer surely someone would have mentioned it? But they hadn't. They'd only ever said he kept animals and couldn't leave the herd at this time of year. They'd never said anything about *reindeer*!

Thomas pressed his face to the window. He watched as Grandad sorted the animals into pairs and hitched them to an enormous sledge he brought out of the garage. Then he climbed on to the sledge and shook the reins. The reindeer started forward, straining at the harness. Slowly, gradually the sledge began to move, gathering speed as it slid over the snow. As it passed his window Thomas just had time to see that it was laden with presents...

So *that* was the secret!

No wonder the others hadn't worried about coming north for Christmas!

No wonder they'd all thought it so funny when he wanted to let Santa know his change of address!

Because there was no need. Santa knew exactly where he was spending Christmas.

Because Santa was Grandad!

The sledge took off into the sky. Thomas stared upwards, watching as it circled the house. Was Grandad trying to read the message in the snow? Well, it didn't matter if he couldn't. It didn't matter one little bit. A broad grin spread over Thomas's face. Even the rollerblades didn't seem important any more. No presents on earth could compare with the wonderful discovery he'd made tonight.

He'll find out when the time is right, Grandad had said.

Well, now he *had* found out. And the time was exactly right.

Yawning, Thomas climbed into the narrow bed. Suddenly he felt very, very tired. In no time at all he fell asleep.

The Umbr
Tree Fairy

Jean Ure

All year long, the Fairy from the top of the Christmas tree was shut away in a cardboard box, in a small dark cupboard under the stairs. It had frightened her, at the beginning. She had been brought up on a shelf, in a big department store, surrounded by glitter and tinsel and bright lights. The first time she was locked up she thought she must have done something wrong, and that no one loved her any more.

But that had been many long years ago: she was used to it by now. She knew that for eleven months she must stay in her box, but that for just four wonderful weeks of the year she would be set free.

How the Fairy looked forward to those four weeks! The children would come to the cupboard and take the box into the front room. The lid would be opened and loving hands would lift the

Fairy out. Her skirt would be smoothed, her hair patted into place, her tinsel crown set straight, her broken wand repaired. Somehow, during those long dark months, her wand always managed to get a bit bent and battered, but the children never minded. She was their Fairy and they loved her!

And then, the big moment … one of the children would clamber on to a chair and fix her to the topmost branches of the tree, for everyone to admire. There she would stay for four glorious weeks, enjoying the sights and sounds of Christmas, all the fun and the laughter. She did so miss company when she was locked away in her box in the cupboard!

Not that the Fairy was alone in her cardboard box. She shared it with some Christmas bells and Chinese lanterns, with assorted tree decorations and two glass angels, and an Easter bunny who was only let out at Easter. But Christmas bells were silly tinkly things, and the Chinese lanterns couldn't speak English, while the assorted decorations had no conversation at all and the Angels were simply snooty and stuck-up. They were jealous of her, of course, because she went right to the top of the tree whereas they had to make do with the lower branches. One of these days they would probably get broken, and serve them right!

The Fairy's only real friend was the Easter bunny. He was an easygoing sort of chap, though getting on a bit, now. He had been there when the Fairy first came. He knew a trick or two, did the Easter bunny. He was the only one who had the strength to lift the lid of the box, just a tiny chink, so that whenever the door of the cupboard was opened he could peer out and report what was going on. It was always the Easter bunny who told them when Christmas was about to happen.

"They're preparing for the tree," he would say. (He knew when they were preparing for the tree because the children's mother would reach into the cupboard and take out the big red tub that it stood in.) "Any minute now it'll be your turn!"

And then the Christmas bells would start jingling with excitement and the Chinese lanterns would start babbling together in Chinese and the assorted decorations would start jumping up and down and the Angels would snap at them to "Watch what you're doing, can't you!" because the Angels lived in fear of being broken. The Fairy might have felt some sympathy towards them if they hadn't been so horrid to her.

"She's just a bauble … a mere pagan bauble. *We* have Religious Significance."

It was because they were jealous: the Fairy knew this. But it was still rather hurtful. Nobody wanted to be a mere pagan bauble!

"Don't you worry your pretty little head about it," said the Easter bunny. "You're still the most beautiful thing in the cupboard!"

So year after year, as the children grew up, the Fairy would be placed at the top of the tree and the Angels would be stuck on the lower branches, and the bells and the lanterns and the assorted decorations would be scattered here and there, and every year was just as wonderful as the year which had gone before.

Until one terrible year when tragedy struck.

"They're preparing for the tree," reported the Easter bunny. "Any minute now it'll be your turn!"

The cardboard box instantly became alive. The bells jingled, the lanterns babbled, the decorations jumped up and down. The Angels snapped "Watch out!" and the Fairy put up a hand and patted at her hair. She hated to be all crumpled and untidy, though the children would soon set her to rights.

And then the door of the cupboard opened and the older child, who was called Tanya, picked up the box. The Angels clung to each other as Tanya ran triumphantly into the front room.

"I've got it, Mum!"

The Fairy's heart began to pound. This was her moment – the moment she had waited for all year long! Tanya ripped the lid off the box. She snatched at the Angels.

"Careful," warned her mum. "They're fragile!"

The Angels looked down at the Fairy and smirked. They had never been picked out first before!

The other child, who was called Kate, pulled at a string of Chinese lanterns. Tanya grabbed a handful of assorted decorations. Kate yanked at the bells. Now there were only the Fairy and the

Easter bunny left, and the Easter bunny didn't come out until Easter.

A hand reached in and picked up the Fairy by her hair.

"Ugh! Mum! This old fairy's getting really tatty!"

A shiver of shock ran through the Fairy. One of the Angels sniggered.

"We can't put this on the tree, Mum! Look at it!"

"It's all moth-eaten!"

"It *smells*."

Now the other Angel was sniggering, as well. The Fairy's heart almost stopped beating. What did they mean, tatty? What did they mean, she smelt?

The children's mum picked her up and sniffed at her.

"Mm … a bit musty."

"It's disgusting! It's coming to pieces!"

It was true that the Fairy's dress was rather torn and ragged. That was because one of the Angels had spitefully poked a finger through it. But it could be mended!

"We need a new one, Mum! Can't we have a new one?"

"They've got some in Allders, Mum. Much nicer than this."

"Oh, all right." The children's mother laughed. "You win! It is Christmas, after all." She looked at the Fairy and shook her head. "I'm afraid this poor creature's had it … I wouldn't even give her to charity."

With that, she tossed the Fairy into the waste-paper basket. There the Fairy stayed for the rest of the day, stunned by the terrible thing that had happened to her. Helplessly she lay on her back and watched as the Angels and the bells and the Chinese lanterns were hung about the tree. Later on, the children and their mother went into town to buy a new fairy to replace her. While they were gone, the Angels took the opportunity to jeer.

"She's had *her* day."

"Not even good enough for charity!"

"And she *smells*."

The poor Fairy couldn't even seek comfort from the Easter bunny, because he had been taken back to the cupboard.

After a while, she heard the children return.

"This one's ever so much better, Mum!"

"This one's really ace!"

"So she should be," said the children's mother, "the price I had to pay!"

There was the sound of ripping, of paper being scrunched, and then darkness descended on the waste-paper basket. The Fairy found herself covered in bits of cardboard and plastic so that she never saw the new fairy, the ace fairy who took her place at the top of the tree. Perhaps it was just as well. It would only have upset her.

That night, the children's mother took the waste-paper basket and emptied it into the dustbin. It was cold in the dustbin. It was damp, too; and slimy. The Fairy lay shivering, amongst horrible slippy sloppy bits of this and that. Squeezed oranges: old tea bags: cabbage leaves.

Tears rolled down her cheeks. That she should have come to this! She, who had been the pride of her shelf in the department store! She, who had been so loved! How could they do such a thing to her? She couldn't help being old and tatty.

Sometime during the night, the dustbin was

raided by a family of foxes in search of food. One of the foxes, who was still quite young, pulled out the Fairy and ran off with her into the street. He played with her for a while, tossing her up and down and chasing her, but then his mother called to him and he ran off, leaving the Fairy behind, in the gutter.

There she lay, unseen, for many hours. It rained, and she got wet. The traffic thundered past and terrified her. A bicycle ran over her wand and crushed it. Her skirt was torn and grimy, her hair was matted, her tinsel crown had disappeared. If the Angels could have seen her, they would have laughed so much they would have splintered themselves.

All hope had gone. It was only a matter of time before she was swept up with the rubbish and thrown on to a Council tip.

And then a boy came walking past, his eyes glued to the gutter. The boy was called Tom and he always walked with his eyes glued to the gutter because you never knew what you might find there.

The other day, for instance, he had found an old umbrella that someone had thrown away. The umbrella was broken, but that didn't bother Tom. He had taken it home and stripped off all the material, until there were only the spokes left, and then he had covered the spokes in cooking foil, so that they were like silver branches, and he had stuck it in an empty paint pot, which he had wrapped in shiny red paper, and hung it all about with bits of tinsel until it looked (almost) like a real Christmas tree.

He had found the paint pot in a rubbish skip and the shiny red paper in a waste bin in the High Street. The cooking foil he had collected, painstakingly, day by day, from outside a local restaurant. The restaurant used it for baking potatoes, so that by the time it reached Tom it was all screwed up and sometimes a bit messy, but Tom just took it home and scrubbed it until in the end it was as good as new.

The tinsel was the only thing he had had to buy. It was amazing what you could find if you looked hard enough.

Last year, when Dad had been with them, there hadn't been any need to go out finding things. But Dad was with someone else, now, and Tom and his mum and Tom's little sister were living in one room in what was called a "bed-and-breakfast" and if Tom hadn't gone out and found things there wouldn't have been any Christmas decorations at all. His little sister, whose name was Joely, thought the umbrella tree was pretty as could be. She didn't mind not having a real one. All that was missing was a fairy to go on the top. There'd been a few tears about the fairy. A Christmas tree wasn't a Christmas tree, wept Joely, without a fairy on the top!

Tom's mum had scolded her and told her not to be so ungrateful – "Just look at that lovely tree Tom's made you!" – but Tom didn't think she was being ungrateful. She was only five years old, after all. At five years old you didn't understand why you couldn't have the things that other children took for granted. Tom understood, because Tom was nearly ten. He didn't like it, but he understood. That was why he walked about with his eyes glued to the gutter. He knew his mum couldn't afford to buy Christmas trees and fairies. It was up to Tom to find them.

And there in the gutter was the very thing he was looking for! Tom squatted down and plucked the Fairy out of her puddle. Oh, what a sorry sight! Wet, limp, bedraggled: chewed by a fox, run over by a bicycle. Old and tatty and long past her sell-by date. But still a fairy!

Clutching her in one hand, Tom ran all the way home. Through the doors of the bed-and-breakfast, up the stairs, along the corridor, into the room that he shared with his mum and Joely.

"What have you got there?" said his mum. (Joely was downstairs playing with her friend Dawn, who lived on the floor below. That was good! Tom wanted this to be a surprise.)

"Got a fairy," said Tom.

His mum pulled a face. "It's filthy," she said.

"Gonna wash it," said Tom.

He tore off the Fairy's ruined skirt, fetched a bowl of warm water from the bathroom down the corridor and dunked her in it. Oh, how lovely it was to feel all the horrid grime and the smell of cabbage leaves floating away! The Fairy began to feel almost like a fairy again. (She had been starting to feel like a piece of rubbish.)

Next, Tom dried her very carefully on a towel, and fluffed up her poor thin hair with his mum's hairbrush. After that he mended her wand with sticky tape and snipped a length of tinsel off the umbrella tree to make her a crown. Then his mum, very daring, took the scissors to the net curtains (which were all hanging in tatters anyway) and stitched her a brand-new skirt and top.

"There!" she said. "That's better!"

Tom's mum hid the Fairy in a suitcase under her bed, and that night, when Joely was asleep, she took her out and tied her with a strip of tinsel to the top of the umbrella tree. It was a bit of a come-down, being at the top of an umbrella tree in a bed-and-breakfast when you were used to being at the top of a real tree in a proper house, but somehow the Fairy didn't mind. She was warm, she was dry, she was clean, she was safe. At least, she was for the moment. After the dreadful things that had happened to her, she was no longer sure that she could trust what tomorrow might bring. Maybe these children, also, would decide she was too old and tatty and throw her in the dustbin. A tear rolled down the Fairy's cheek. All she wanted was to be loved!

Next morning, the child that was called Joely woke up early, while it was still dark. She switched on the bedside light and looked up at the umbrella tree. Her eyes went round as saucepan lids. She leaned across to her brother and shook him.

"Tom, Tom! Look!"

Tom woke up with a start. "What?"

"There's a fairy! A beautiful fairy on the tree!"

"So there is," said Tom. "Good old Father Christmas! You see? He *does* listen!"

The Fairy was greatly admired. Joely's friend, Dawn, came upstairs to look at her.

"I wish I had a fairy like that," she said.

"You can't have this one," said Joely. "She's mine. But you can share her," she added.

That night, when they went to bed, Joely seemed rather anxious. Looking up at the Fairy, she said,

"Will she still be there in the morning?"

"You bet," said Tom.

"Tom, *is* she mine? Is she mine to keep?"

"For just as long as you want her," said Tom.

"I want her for ever," whispered Joely. "For ever and ever!"

And so the Fairy stayed with Joely for ever and ever. She is there with her still – and she doesn't have to live in a box in the dark any more because Joely takes her to bed with her every night.

Just now and again, the Fairy thinks back and remembers her old life, with the glass angels and the jingling bells and the children called Tanya and Kate. She no longer misses any of it, though she does sometimes wonder how the Easter bunny is getting on. Probably, knowing him, he is busy making up to the new fairy. He was always one for a pretty face!

But if ever he grows too old and is thrown out with the rubbish, the Fairy hopes with all her heart that a boy like Tom will find him.

Sparrow's Special Christmas

Susan Gates

I'm in a really bad mood! Christmas is cancelled. There isn't going to be a Christmas this year.

We're snowed in! When I woke up this morning the whole world was white. We couldn't believe it. Even the weather girl on telly couldn't believe it: "It really took us by surprise," she said.

"I hate you, snow!" I told it. I even shook my fist out of the window at it.

Tomorrow is *supposed* to be Christmas Day. But we haven't got any crackers or Christmas pudding yet. And we haven't got my new bike! Dad was *supposed* to be collecting it from the town today. But now he can't get through to the shops. Not even on the tractor. We've got to wait for the snow ploughs to dig us out.

I asked Mum, "Why do you always have to leave

things until the last minute? Why didn't you get my bike before?"

And Mum said, "Because we're so busy. There's so much to do on the farm."

They're always busy. Feeding the sheep, fixing fences, doing all sorts of jobs. They're out there now, seeing if the sheep are all right. They don't have time for Christmas.

And I'm stuck here with Gran. She always comes to our house for Christmas.

"Lucky I got here before the snow," she says. "Or I wouldn't have got here at all."

I just grunt, "*Harumph!*" I'm in such a bad mood. Bet all my friends are having a *proper* Christmas. Bet *their* mums and dads did the shopping on time.

Crash! The front door bursts open. Mum staggers in. She looks like an Arctic explorer, all crusty with snow. Her eyelashes are frozen! They look like they're threaded with little glass beads.

"*Burrr*," she says, pulling off her boots. "It's dreadful out there!"

"You mean you can't get to the shops?" I ask her.

"We were lucky to get to the top field," she says.

"It's really, really bad. Your dad's trying to get the sheep in now."

Gran says, "I haven't seen a Christmas like this since 1947. In 1947 me and your grandad had Fold House Farm. And we were snowed up there. We had to warm the Christmas lambs up in the bottom of the big oven. It was the only way to keep them alive."

I give a big yawn. I know it's rude but I can't help it. I've heard this story before – about warming the Christmas lambs in the big oven. We don't do that kind of thing nowadays. We've got special incubator things to warm up Christmas lambs. They work with electricity.

Mum says: "It's getting worse out there!"

"Oh no!" I say. "What a horrible, horrible Christmas. Didn't you even get me some sweets – a selection box or something?"

"No," says my mum. "We were going to do most of our Christmas shopping today. We were even going to collect the turkey today. I'm really, really sorry, Sparrow."

My mum and dad always call me Sparrow. It's

not my real name of course. Katherine's my real name.

"Look, Sparrow," says Mum, suddenly. "I've got something to show you."

Maybe she did get a present after all!

But it isn't a present. It's a catalogue. Mum opens it and says, "There's the bike we've got you, Sparrow. I know it's not the same as your real present. But at least you can look at a picture of it."

I'm so mad, I refuse to look at the picture.

"What kind of a Christmas present is that?" I shout at Mum. "A stupid picture? I can't ride around on a picture, can I? I want my proper Christmas present! Not just a stupid picture!"

And do you know what I do next? Throw the catalogue in the waste-paper bin, that's what I do. I know I'm acting like a little kid. But I just can't help it. Christmas should be really nice. Christmas should be just perfect.

"At least you've got a Christmas tree," says Gran. "Look how pretty the lights are."

Then guess what happens? The Christmas tree lights go out.

I can't believe it! One second they're bright and twinkly. The next they're dead.

"Oh, no," sighs Mum. "Not a power cut! The snow must have brought the wires down."

That's all I need. No presents, no sweets, no turkey. And now no Christmas television. This is going to be the worst Christmas ever!

It's Christmas morning. When I wake up the first thing I do is shiver, "*Burrr!*" There's still no electricity. My radiator is freezing cold. When I breathe out, "*Huuuhh!*" my breath makes little white clouds.

There's a bright white light coming through my curtains. I know what that means. It means the snow's still there. Last night I dreamed it had all melted away. And my dad got through to town – five minutes before the bike shop closed. And when I went downstairs on Christmas morning there was a bike-shaped parcel, under the Christmas tree.

Who am I kidding? When I look outside the snow is worse then ever.

"I hate you, snow!" I say, out loud. I make a hideous face at it, through the window.

Might as well stay in bed. There's nothing to get up for. I'm just snuggling back into my duvet when Gran calls from downstairs.

"Katherine, are you awake?"

Gran never calls me Sparrow, she always calls me Katherine.

Her voice sounds a bit worried so I wrap myself in my duvet and get out of bed.

"Ow!" The floor's icy cold.

"Ow!" I've just fallen over my shepherd's crook. It's the one I had for the school Christmas play. Every year I'm a shepherd! Just because I live on a farm. I'm sick of it. Why can't I be an angel for a change? Why can't I have big, silver wings?

I drag myself downstairs in my duvet. Gran's in the kitchen lighting a fire in the old fireplace.

"Pet Sheep hasn't come to the kitchen door," she says.

I haven't told you about Pet Sheep. Sometimes, on the farm, we get a lamb whose mother dies or is too sick to feed it. So we feed the lamb with a bottle. And it gets really tame and it gets used to us. And we call it our Pet Lamb. And when it grows up we call it our Pet Sheep. We've got a Pet Sheep now and she's always hanging round the kitchen door. She lives in the little paddock by the barn. And she comes to the back door for food. She likes Polo mints but don't tell Mum I feed her those. Today, because it's Christmas Day, I was going to give her a whole tube of Polo mints for a present. They're on the mantelpiece, wrapped in silver foil, all ready for her. But she hasn't come to get them.

"Where are Mum and Dad?" I ask Gran. "Have you told them about Pet Sheep?"

"They're digging out sheep in the top field," says Gran. "I hope they're all right. This snow is really bad."

I forget about feeling grumpy. Suddenly, there's a sick, shivery feeling inside my stomach.

"They will be all right, won't they, Gran?" I ask her.

Gran doesn't answer my question. Her face looks grim and serious. She just says, "Katherine, I haven't seen a Christmas as bad as this since 1947."

It doesn't feel like Christmas. Christmas should be warm and bright and sparkly. But our house is cold and gloomy. And I'm worried about Pet Sheep and worried about Mum and Dad, out there in the snowdrifts.

Then I remember something else that makes me even more worried.

"Pet Sheep is going to lamb soon," I tell Gran. "But it's not until next week."

"You sometimes get early lambs," says Gran. "Sometimes they come when you don't expect them."

"Don't say that, Gran. She can't have her lamb now. Not in all this snow!"

The paddock is only across the farmyard. You can see it from the back door. But the farmyard is full of deep, deep snow. It's as high as our kitchen windows.

"We must get to Pet Sheep," I tell Gran desperately. "She might need our help!"

Then Gran starts one of her stories. I can't

believe it! This is an emergency! Pet Sheep might be buried under a snowdrift. She might be having an early lamb. All on her own, in this weather. And my Grandma's telling stories about olden times!

"In 1947," says Gran, "in that bad winter, our sheep got buried under snowdrifts. And I was really skinny then, just like I am now. I didn't weigh much at all. Your grandad said I was light as a feather. And do you know, if you don't weigh much you can walk on snowdrifts, you don't sink in."

I was going to yawn. But I stop myself, just in time. And I start listening to Gran's story. I mean, *really* listening.

"I went out to find the sheep," Gran tells me. "I walked on top of the snowdrifts. I had a long stick and every three steps I poked it into the snow to see if a sheep was buried."

"How did you know when you'd found one?" I ask her.

"They wriggle," says Gran. "When you poke them with a stick, they wriggle, under the snow."

Why didn't I think of that? I'm getting excited now.

"I could walk on the snowdrifts," I tell Gran. "I could do that! I don't weigh much. That's why my dad calls me Sparrow."

"You're not going," says Gran sternly. "If anyone's going, I'm going!"

"I'm coming too. It's my Pet Sheep!"

Gran frowns.

"I'm lighter than you!" I tell her.

"All right," says Gran. "You can come. At least I can keep an eye on you."

I throw off my duvet: "Let's get ready then!"

We get ready in double-quick time. Socks, jumpers, trousers, wellies, gloves, hats. We look like big, fat caterpillars when we've finished.

"And now," says Gran, "we need a long stick."

We look round the kitchen.

"I know!" I tell Gran. "I know what we'll use!"

I clump upstairs in my wellies and grab my shepherd's crook. You know, I'm glad now I wasn't an angel this year. I clump downstairs again.

"Perfect," says Gran when she sees my crook. "That's just what we need."

"Wait," I tell Gran. I clump over to the mantelpiece. Pet Sheep's Christmas present is there – the tube of Polo mints, all wrapped up. I stick it in my coat pocket.

Gran picks up a spade from beside the kitchen door. "We might need this," she says.

We're ready now. Ready to go on a rescue mission to find Pet Sheep!

"I'll test the snow first," says Gran.

And then she does this amazing thing! She opens the kitchen window. She climbs up on to the sofa. And she walks out of the window. She walks right out on to the snow! Just like that!

She bounces up and down on it, as if it's a trampoline! It goes, squeak, squeak, under her wellies. But she doesn't sink in.

"It's nice and firm," says Gran. "You can come out now."

So I climb out of the window too.

And we're walking on top of snowdrifts, me and Gran! The snow's crunchy and creaky but we don't sink. The sun comes out and makes the snow bright and sparkly. And it's really Christmassy. It's brilliant. It's like walking on top of a giant Christmas cake!

But then I start worrying about Pet Sheep.

I'm getting cold now. *Clack, clack, clack.* What's that noise? It's my teeth.

"Here's the paddock, Gran!"

We nearly missed it. Because all you can see is the top of the paddock wall, poking above the snow.

"Start sliding the crook in," says Gran. "Gently, gently," she warns. "And try close to the wall. That's where sheep like to shelter."

I slide in my shepherd's crook. Did something wriggle? Or is it me shivering?

"No," says Gran. She's listening hard. Listening for scuffling sounds deep under the snow. "Nothing there. Try this place here."

We try and try. We scrunch round the paddock. And every three steps we poke another hole. But we don't find anything. Nothing wriggles under the snow.

I'm so cold and tired I'm nearly crying. The sun has gone in. "More snow on the way," says Gran, looking at the grey clouds.

"We'll never find Pet Sheep!" I say.

And I nearly give up. But my little gran doesn't give up. She doesn't seem to feel the cold. She's tough, my gran. She can chuck hay bales about. I've seen her. Not many grans can do that.

"Let's try over there," she says.

I trudge after her. I've got three pairs of socks on but my toes are like ice-pops. I've got gloves on but my fingers are stinging like mad and I want to go back and…

Whoops! I've tripped over something. I crash to my knees and my hand reaches out and grabs something: "Urgh, what's that?" It's wool, all crispy with ice.

"Pet Sheep!" I cry. "It's Pet Sheep!"

Pet Sheep isn't buried very deep. I start digging like mad with my hands like a dog digging up a bone. There's snow flying all around. But Gran gently pushes me out the way. I forgot she'd brought a spade.

Very carefully, she starts to dig. And soon I see Pet Sheep's head.

"She's all right. Look, she's all right."

"Baaa!" says Pet Sheep.

"Come with us, girl," I tell Pet Sheep. "You're only a little sheep. You can walk on the snow too."

But Pet Sheep doesn't move. She doesn't wriggle free. She just stays in her hole in the snow.

I unwrap her Christmas present. "Come on girl, come on!" I hold out a Polo. But even a Polo mint won't make her follow me.

"I think I know what's wrong," says Gran.

Gently, very gently, she clears more snow away. She does it with her hands, not the spade. And she finds a soggy little bundle.

I peer into the hole in the snow: "It's a lamb!"

"She won't come without her lamb," says Gran.

Gran lifts out the lamb and it's floppy. Its legs are all dangly.

"Is it dead?" I ask her.

"Nearly," says Gran. "We'd better hurry back."

As fast as we can, we start plodding back to the house. I carry the crook and the spade. Gran hugs the lamb to her coat. Pet Sheep scrambles out of the hole and comes trotting after us.

It's starting to snow again. Big soft flakes that stick to your face.

"Hurry!" says Gran, urgently.

I can't see where we're going. The world is all white and whirling. But Gran knows the way. And soon we're crawling back through the kitchen window.

"What about Pet Sheep?"

Pet Sheep pokes her head through the window: "Baaaa!"

"Leave her outside," says Gran. "We'll see to her in a minute. It's her lamb I'm worried about."

The lamb's eyes are closed.

"We'll have to warm it up," says Gran.

"I'll get the incubator!" I go racing off. I know where it is. It's in the storeroom, under the stairs.

Then I remember, "Oh no!"

There's no electricity.

Gran takes the lamb close to the fire. But it still looks dead. "Poor little mite," says Gran.

I nearly ask: "What did you do in 1947, Gran?" But then I remember. They warmed lambs up in the bottom of the big oven. And guess what? Our oven's electric.

But my gran isn't beaten yet.

"Have you got any baking foil?" she asks me. "You know, the silver kind, that comes on a roll?"

"Yes, we have!"

I know we have because my mum's got some extra-wide foil for the Christmas turkey. But we couldn't collect the turkey so we don't need it any more, do we?

I grab the foil from a cupboard and Gran tears off a big piece. Then she wraps the lamb in it!

"That'll keep it warm," she says.

My gran's a genius. She really is.

"Have you got a cardboard box?"

"There's the box that we keep the Christmas tree decorations in."

"That'll do."

So we put the lamb in the box. It looks like a Christmas present, all done up in silver wrapping. We put the box by the fire. Then we sit and wait.

"Baa!" goes Pet Sheep outside the window. She's worried about her baby.

"It's all right, Pet Sheep!" I call out to her in a cheerful voice. "You can have your baby back in a minute. But we've got to warm it up first!"

But I don't feel cheerful. The lamb isn't moving at all.

"Please let it be alive!" I wish. "Please let it be alive. It'd be the best Christmas present ever!"

But the lamb still doesn't move.

Gran shakes her head. "It's been out in the cold too long," she says, sadly.

I feel really sad too. As if there's a heavy stone inside me. I get up from the fire. I drag myself over to the window one … step … at … a … time. I don't want to do it. But I've got to. I've got to tell Pet Sheep what's happened.

"Hang on a minute," says Gran.

She peers into the box. I rush back and peer into the box too.

The silver foil's going all crinkly, as if there's something twitching inside it.

"Maaa!" says the lamb, in a tiny voice. "Maaa!"

The front door crashes open. A gust of snow blows in. And there are Mum and Dad. They've come back safe from the snowdrifts! They're stomping around to keep warm. Slapping the snow off their clothes.

"Are you all right, Sparrow?" asks Dad.

"Dad! We've rescued Pet Sheep. Me and Gran did it. We walked on the snowdrifts. We dug her out. She's got a lamb! And look, it's still alive!"

I'm in bed, wrapped in my duvet. I'm warm because I've got two hot-water bottles. Christmas Day is nearly over.

What a funny Christmas Day! It wasn't a proper Christmas. We didn't have crackers or turkey or a selection box. We ate soup warmed up on the fire. Then we warmed up tinned rice pudding for afters.

But Pet Sheep's lamb grew stronger and stronger. She was going, "MAAA! MAAA!" while we ate our Christmas dinner. She was standing up on wobbly legs. As soon as we knew she was all right we gave her back to Pet Sheep. They're out in the barn, with lots of hay to keep them warm. So I've got a Pet Sheep and Pet Lamb now. Wonder if Pet Lamb likes Polos as much as her mum?

You know that catalogue that I threw away? With the picture of my Christmas bike in it? Well, I went to get it out of the waste-paper bin. It was all crumpled up so I smoothed it out. And do you know what? It's a beautiful silver bike. I can't wait to get it. I've cut the picture out and put it under my pillow. But I keep taking it out and putting my torch on so I can have another look.

It wasn't a *proper* Christmas. But it was a special Christmas. I'll never forget it. And when I get really old, like Gran, I'll tell everyone about it. About the special Christmas when we had soup for our Christmas dinner. When Gran and me walked on snowdrifts and dug out Pet Sheep. And saved Pet Lamb's life by wrapping her in silver foil that was meant for the Christmas turkey!

The Pirates'
Christmas Party

Adèle Geras

"After you've both finished your pudding," said Beth, "you can listen to what I wrote at school today. It was so good that Mrs Barnes made me read it out in front of the whole class."

"What have we done to deserve it?" said Andy, Beth's brother, and their mother said: "Be quiet, Andy. We listen to you often enough, going on and on about this and that." She smiled at Beth. "We'd love to hear it."

"What's it about?" said Andy, sighing. "Go on, get it over with."

"It's called 'My Best Christmas Present Ever'. Are you ready? I'll stand up so that you can hear me properly."

"We're all together round the table," said Mum. "We're not in the Albert Hall. I think you can stay sitting down."

"I'll go and get it out of my school bag then," said Beth. "Don't anybody move."

She was back almost at once, holding a big sheet of paper. Andy groaned.

"It's not long, is it?" he said. "Some of us have got stuff to do."

"It's as long as it has to be," said Beth, "to say what I want it to say."

"Get on with it then," said Andy.

"Right," said Beth. "I will." She coughed and sat up very straight in her chair:

"'My Best Christmas Present Ever' by Beth Johnston. Class 4.

"'My dad works on an oil-rig, and last year he had to stay on the rig over Christmas. He sent me a present from Scotland. It is a ship in a bottle. The ship is called a galleon. My dad says that ships are always called "she", like girls. She has three masts and lovely white sails, and a figurehead of a red fish with blue eyes. She is very beautiful. My brother Andrew is ten years old, and he likes pirates. He said she was a pirate ship. Dad said I could call her anything I wanted, so I decided on "The Crimson Cod". I put the bottle with the ship in it on the table next to my bed, and when I go to sleep, I wish I could get very tiny and wake up on board the galleon, as a cabin-girl.'

"There." Beth beamed at her mother and brother. "What did you think of that?"

"Not bad," said Andy, "and quite short, really."

"It was lovely!" said Mum. "Keep it to show Dad when he gets back tomorrow. Now, who's going to help me with the dishes?"

The last thing Beth did before she got into bed was open a door on her advent calendar. December 14th. Tomorrow was the last day of school. There would be turkey and roast potatoes in the canteen, and everyone singing carols in the afternoon. Then came the ten days before Christmas: the best ten days of the year. Beth loved choosing gifts and making decorations and finding exactly the right tree, and writing Christmas cards and wrapping all the presents in special paper covered with pictures of Santa and his reindeer. She longed to make a snowman, and wished they lived in a colder part of the country.

Beth spent a lot of time wishing and when she wasn't wishing, she was imagining. Sometimes she pretended she was a princess, and sometimes that she was one of King Arthur's knights. Sometimes she imagined that she lived in the dolls' house under the window, and was friends with all her dolls, but the very best games of all were the ones she played with Andy. He didn't play with her as often as she would have liked, but the Pirate Game was Beth's favourite. Andy said that "Andrew" wasn't a very piratical name, so he became Captain Cutlass Caleb and she was his trusty cabin-girl, Buccaneer Beth.

She lay in bed and turned on her side so that she could look at the Crimson Cod, safe in her bottle. Someone had painted green and blue waves on the glass, so that it really looked as though the little galleon were flying through the water. Perhaps, thought Beth, they were on their way to search for buried treasure. She closed her eyes. Suddenly, it seemed as though her whole bed was rocking gently to and fro…

Beth sat up. She blinked and rubbed her eyes. Where was her bedroom? What had happened to her bed? And why wasn't she wearing her pyjamas with spacemen on them? She seemed to be in a hammock, in a long, low room, dimly lit by one lantern. There were other hammocks, slung from beams in the ceiling, and in them Beth could see...

"Pirates!" she cried aloud, and rolled out of her hammock and on to the floor. "You're all pirates! I'm on a pirate ship. Wake up, please! Help!" She could hear snores all around her.

She peered into the nearest hammock and saw a pink-faced man with a long, ginger beard, sleeping with his mouth open. She prodded him.

"Avast, me hearties..." he mumbled, and opened his eyes. "Oh, 'tis you, Buccaneer Beth. Pass me the rum, there's a good cabin-girl."

"Who are you?" asked Beth. The ginger beard shook and wobbled while the pirate laughed.

"I'm Ginger George," he said, "as well you know, Beth m'dear." The other pirates began to wake up. Beth decided to watch and listen and pretend that she knew exactly what was going on. I'm dreaming, she said to herself. I was looking at the Crimson Cod before I fell asleep and now I'm dreaming that I'm aboard a pirate ship. I shall wake up soon, so I'm not going to worry.

Breakfast on board a pirate ship turned out to be hard biscuits dipped in cold beer.

"Don't you have cornflakes?" Beth asked Ginger George. "Or toast and marmalade?"

"Them's for landlubbers," said Fearsome Four-Eye Fergal, a skinny pirate who wore glasses and didn't seem fearsome at all.

After breakfast, Beth followed the others up on deck.

" 'Tis time," said Fergal, "to swab the decks and mizzen the main mast and swizzle the sails." Beth had never heard of swizzling the sails, so she pointed to a small, round man in a red coat. He had an eye-patch and a long twirly moustache. Beth said:

"Is that the Captain?"

"You know it is," Fergal answered. "That's Black-Hearted Basil, the Scourge of the Seven Seas and Captain of the Crimson Cod."

"Are we sailing on the Crimson Cod?" Beth wanted to know.

"You're asking more daft questions than there's weevils in the flour, lass. Surely you know what your own ship is called?"

Beth said nothing. A terrible thought occurred to her. What if she weren't dreaming? What if there really *was* such a thing as wishes coming true? What if she truly *was* on board a pirate ship? Would she ever get back to her real life? For a moment she felt like crying. I'm never going to make a wish again, she said to herself. And what about Christmas? She said to Fergal: "Are we going to do anything exciting for Christmas?"

"Never do," said Fergal. "Not as long as I've been at sea."

"No presents?"

"No."

"No turkey or mince pies?"

"No."

"Don't you hang out your stockings on Christmas Eve?" Fergal shook his head.

"What about singing carols?"

"We sing sea-shanties," said Fergal. "Never heard of no carols."

"I wish," said Beth, "to see the Captain."

"The Captain's a busy man," said Fergal. "I doubt he'll have the time to bandy words with the likes o' you."

Beth, however, was quite determined to speak to Black-Hearted Basil and so Fergal led her to his cabin door. She knocked on it three times.

"Enter!" said a pleasant, rather soft voice.

Beth opened the door, and tried not to stare. Black-Hearted Basil was sitting on a sofa, knitting. Beside him was a gigantic white, fluffy cat who looked just like a round cushion that had had two green eyes sewn on to it. All around the cabin were straw baskets overflowing with balls of wool in every colour you could possibly imagine, and there was an embroidery frame in one corner, where Basil had just started work on a tapestry. The picture painted on the canvas was of a country cottage and a garden full of flowers. Beth looked at it in amazement.

"You're admiring my tapestry, I see," said Basil.

"It's a new hobby of mine. I've only ever done knitting and crochet before, so I thought I'd branch out."

"I never knew," said Beth, "that pirates did things like knitting."

"Well, the days at sea are endlessly long, my duck, and there's only so much swabbing and mizzening and shinning up the rigging that a chap can do all at once."

"But what about boarding other ships and stealing their cargo? Burying treasure and making maps of where it's to be found? What about making people walk the plank?" Beth sounded quite plaintive.

"Oh, we do all those things occasionally of course. When the need arises, you might say. But it does still leave me an awful lot of time to pursue my hobbies. Do you like what I'm making now?" He held up his knitting so that Beth could see it better. "It's a fiendishly difficult Fair Isle pattern, but this waistcoat will be a thing of beauty, mark my words."

Beth coughed. If she didn't say something soon, the Captain would keep her there discussing knitting patterns for ages. She said:

"Please, sir, I'd like to organize a Christmas party."

"Christmas?" The Captain counted off a few stitches and muttered to himself for a moment. "Is it Christmas already?"

"Yes, sir, and I think we should have a party. We could decorate the ship, and the Cook could make a cake, and we could sing carols. I don't suppose we could get hold of a Christmas tree, but I'm sure everyone would love a party."

The Captain sucked the end of a knitting needle and said: "Decorations … decorations … that rings a bell … I'm sure that somewhere in here…" He smiled at Beth. "Please forgive me. I've been at sea so long that I've forgotten what some of these old chests have actually got in them, only I have a distinct memory of my old mum saying something about Christmas, last time she packed my sea-chests. Let's have a little look."

Black-Hearted Basil laid his knitting down on the sofa.

"Morgan," he said to the cat, "don't you dare

chew my wool." Morgan yawned as though wool-chewing would be altogether too much effort, and closed his eyes for a nap. Black-Hearted Basil began to rummage, first in one chest, then in another.

"Here we are!" he cried at last. "I knew it! Here's enough decorations for an entire fleet of ships!"

Beth couldn't believe her eyes. There were rolls of tinsel, coloured glass balls, paper lanterns, yards and yards of red ribbon, little bottles full of glitter, a bag full of assorted gold and silver stars, plastic holly and mistletoe, and right at the bottom of the chest, a little Christmas tree, carefully wrapped up in a polythene bag.

"That's my mum all over," said Basil. "She thinks of everything. Real Christmas trees shed their needles all over the carpet, but this little imitation one … well, it's quite lovely, don't you agree?"

"It's perfect," said Beth. "Now we can have a really wonderful Christmas party. I shall go and talk to the Cook at once."

"And I shall summon the crew on to the deck and address them all. I don't do that very often and

I shall enjoy it. Come and listen, before you go down and talk to Cook."

Beth and the Captain went up on deck. The First Mate, Desperate Bertie, rang the bell that called the pirates from every corner of the Crimson Cod. When they had all gathered into a raggedy crowd, Black-Hearted Basil raised his hand for silence.

"Our esteemed cabin-girl, Buccaneer Beth, has had a splendid idea. We are going to have a Christmas Party!"

The crew cheered loudly, and several of the pirates threw their caps in the air and whistled.

"Now," the Captain continued, "has anyone got anything at all Christmassy tucked away in their sea-going bundles? I want you all to have a good look and tell young Beth what you come up with... We will all assemble here again in one hour."

The pirates hurried away to look through their belongings. After an hour, they came up on deck once more, and Beth made a list of everything they had found. The list read:

1 box of assorted crackers - ~~Peg-leg Percy~~.

2 boxes of mixed streamers - Browntooth Billy.

1 set of angel chimes (with candles) - One-arm Eric

3 sets of paper napkins (holly and bells pattern)
- Jabez the Knife.

1 fairy doll (for top of tree) - Silent Angus.

1 Santa Claus costume - Ginger George.

1 mouth organ - Fearsome Fergal.

"That's a very good list," said Beth. "Thank you all very much indeed."

"I'll tell you what I've found," said Desperate Bertie, "and that's a bundle of knitted stockings. The Captain tried to interest me in knitting, aargh, a good few years ago now, but I only ever got the hang of stockings. P'raps we can hang 'em on our hammocks, come Christmas Eve, and Ginger George can dress up in that there costume of his, and fill 'em all with ship's biscuits!"

"What a good idea, Bertie!" said Beth. "Please go and find them. Each man at the party can have one and that will be their going-home present. You can't have a proper party without a present to take home. We'll get Ginger George to give them out."

The next few hours were spent in frantic preparations. Cross-Eyed Colin, the Cook of the Crimson Cod, (who never left his kitchen, even in a Force Ten gale) had been persuaded to open his secret larder, and in it there were enough good things to make:

1 enormous fruit cake.

24 mince pies.

2 gallons of brandy sauce.

The younger members of the crew climbed the rigging and tied coloured tinsel to the tops of the sails. They fixed the biggest gold star of all to the very top of the tallest mast, where it caught the sun and twinkled brightly enough to dazzle the passing sea birds. Down on the deck, a big spare sail was unrolled and spread out like a table cloth, and Jabez the Knife (who had once done a three-week course in Flower Arrangement) had decorated the table with sprigs of imitation holly and paper napkins in the shape of roses. There was a cracker beside every plate, and the angel chimes made a pretty centre-piece. The Captain's Christmas tree, with Silent Angus's fairy doll right at the top of it, stood on an upturned bucket, which had been cunningly covered in red crêpe paper to make it look festive. Cross-Eyed Colin ventured up on deck for the first time in years to set out the food, and Beth poured rum into every glass.

When all the pirates had sat down, Beth said:

"The first thing we must do is pull our crackers and put on our paper hats."

This took some time, while the pirates giggled and shrieked and swapped hats with one another, because there were some people who didn't think blue suited them, and others who said they'd rather not wear orange, thank you very much.

Then came the eating and drinking. Everyone agreed it was the best feast ever to be spread on the deck of the Crimson Cod. There wasn't a single pirate who didn't have to loosen his waistband before long, and Ginger George, magnificent in his Santa Claus outfit, began muttering about going on a diet. Beth stood up. She said:

"Thank you all very much for helping to make

this such a lovely party. Before Ginger George gives you all your knitted stockings as a present, I'd like you to join in with this Christmas sea-shanty I've made up. It's very easy to learn."

"Yes!" shouted the pirates. "Sing us a Christmas shanty, lass!"

Beth coughed a little and began to sing:

"Paper hats and a spring of holly,
a cracker to pull with a yo-ho-ho.
Tinsel on the sails looks oh, so jolly.
It's Christmas time, so yo-heave-ho.

Fill our Christmas stockings with nice surprises,
yo-ho-ho and a bell to ring.
Nuts and oranges and fat mince pie-ses.
Sing a Christmas shanty, boys!
Sing, sing, sing!"

Fergal took up the tune on his mouth-organ, and soon all the pirates were singing loudly enough to shiver the timbers of the Crimson Cod.

After the singing, Ginger George went and

found his sack, and the pirates lined up for their gift of one knitted stocking each. Beth said to Bertie:

"They're really beautiful, Bertie. You never told me they were stripy."

"Oh, aye," said Bertie. "Not much point to a stocking, unless it's striped. That's what my Auntie Maud always used to say."

"May I have one as well?" Beth asked.

"Of course," said Ginger George, plunging his hand into the sack. "What do you say to stripes of purple and green?"

"Thank you," said Beth. "I'll keep it as a souvenir of the party."

In the end, even the fiercest pirate has to go to bed. Beth climbed into her hammock, clutching her knitted stocking. The Crimson Cod rocked gently on the waves, and Beth fell asleep almost at once.

Suddenly someone was shouting in her ear.

"Come on, lazy Beth!" said her mum's voice. "School today, you know. You can't lie in until tomorrow."

Beth opened her eyes and knew at once that she was back in her own bedroom.

"I dreamed I was on a pirate ship last night..." she started to say, but Mum was already on her way downstairs.

"Tell me about it later," she called over her shoulder.

Beth washed and dressed. Then she looked down at the Crimson Cod, lying quietly in her glass bottle. Something was glittering at the top of the main mast, and Beth picked up the bottle to have a closer look. There, for anyone to see, was a tiny gold star.

"It *was* true," Beth whispered to herself. "I *did* sail on a pirate ship." She shook her head and blinked her eyes and looked again. The gold star was still there. Maybe she'd tell Andy about it all later. He'd believe her. She didn't think anyone else would. Beth thought: we won't say a word about it to other people ... it'll be our secret, Andy's and mine. She put the bottle with the Crimson Cod in it back on the table and went downstairs smiling to herself.

Later that morning, Beth's mother was tidying up her daughter's room. She found what looked like a doll's stocking on the floor beside the bed. It had been hand-knitted in thin stripes of purple and green. Beth's mum put it away in the dolls' house, wondering, not for the first time, where Beth found some of the things that ended up among her toys.

The Box of Magic

Malorie Blackman

It was Christmas Eve, but Peter was in no hurry. His head bent, Peter dragged his feet as he made his way slowly home. There was no point in rushing. Mum and Dad would only be arguing about something or another. Peter and his sister Chloe had hoped that the quarrelling would stop over Christmas. It hadn't. If anything, it'd got worse.

Peter had spent all afternoon searching and searching for the perfect present for his mum and dad. Something that would stop them quarrelling for just five minutes. Something that would make Christmas the way it used to be, with smiles and songs and happiness in every corner of the house. But all the searching had been for nothing. Peter didn't have that much money to begin with and all the things he could afford, he didn't want. All the gifts he could afford looked so cheap and tacky that Peter knew they would fall apart about ten seconds after they were handled. What was he going to do? He had to buy something and time was running out.

Then he caught sight of it out of the corner of his eye.

The medium-sized sign above the door said "The Christmas Shop" in spidery writing. The small shop window was framed with silver and gold tinsel and a scattering of glitter like mini stars. At the bottom of the window, fake snow had been sprayed. It looked so much like the real thing that had it been outside the window instead of inside, Peter would've been sure it was real snow. A single Christmas tree laden down with fairy lights and baubles and yet more tinsel stood proudly in the exact centre of the window.

Peter stood in front of the shop and stared. He'd never seen anything so … wonderful! It was as if Christmas had started in this shop and then spread out to cover the whole wide world.

"The Christmas Shop…" Peter muttered to himself.

He wondered why he'd never seen it before. True, it was behind the shopping precinct and he usually walked through the precinct not around it, but even so. Peter looked up and down the street. The few other shops in the same row as the Christmas Shop were all boarded up.

Unexpectedly, the shop door opened. A tall portly man with a white beard and a merry twinkle in his eyes stood in the doorway.

"Hello! Come in! Come in!" The shopkeeper beckoned.

"I … er … don't have much money." Peter shook his head.

"No matter. Come in." The shopkeeper turned and held the door open. It was as if there was no doubt in his mind that Peter would enter. Uncertainly, Peter dithered on the pavement. He hadn't intended to go in. He was only window shopping. But the shop looked so warm and inviting and the shopkeeper seemed so friendly. Peter walked into the shop.

And he gasped in amazement!

It was even better inside than it had appeared from outside. It smelt of freshly baked bread and warm cakes and toast and cinnamon and nutmeg and it was so warm it was as if the sun itself had come for a visit.

"Isn't my shop the best!" smiled the shopkeeper. "Look around. Feel free. You can pick up anything, touch anything."

Peter stared at the shopkeeper. He certainly wasn't like any other shopkeeper Peter had ever met. Usually shopkeepers didn't like school kids in their shops and they certainly didn't like them touching things. Peter wandered around the shop, his dark brown eyes wide with delight. Toys and games and Christmas sweets and Christmas treats filled every corner.

Peter's hand curled around the money in his pocket. He could buy all his Christmas presents in here. Peter bent his head to examine a gold and berry-red scarf. That would be perfect for his mum. And maybe the night-blue and yellow scarf for his dad. And he could get that little glass unicorn over there for Chloe. That was just the kind of thing she liked. The strange thing was, none of the items had prices on them.

"H-How much are these woolly scarves?" Peter asked, crossing his fingers in his pockets. "And how much is that unicorn over there?"

"That depends on who they're for and why you think they'd like them," answered the shopkeeper.

"The scarves are for my mum and dad and the unicorn is for my sister. Chloe likes things made of glass. She keeps them in her bedroom on the window sill. And I thought that Mum and Dad could have the scarves to keep them warm."

"And how much money do you have?" asked the shopkeeper.

Peter took out all the money in his pocket. The shopkeeper checked through it carefully.

"You're lucky," said the shopkeeper. "You've got enough for all the things you want."

"I have? Really?" Peter couldn't believe it.

The shopkeeper smiled and nodded. Peter grinned at him, but slowly his smile faded. He'd buy the scarves for his dad and mum and then what? What good would any present do? Peter could see it now. Mum and Dad opening their presents on Christmas Day.

"Thanks Peter. That's great," says Dad.

"Peter, that's wonderful," says Mum.

And then they'd fling their presents to the back of the chair and start shouting at each other again.

"What's the matter, Peter?" asked the shopkeeper gently.

Peter jumped. He'd been lost in a world of his own.

"It's just that... Hang on a second. How did you know my name?" Peter stared.

"It's a little game of mine," the shopkeeper beamed. "I like to guess people's names and nine times out of ten, I get it right."

Peter was impressed.

"So you were saying?" the shopkeeper prompted.

"I ... I don't suppose you've got anything in your shop to stop my mum and dad from fighting?" The moment the words were out of his mouth, Peter regretted it. What was he doing? He hadn't told anyone about his mum and dad, not even his best friend Andy. No one knew how things were at home except his sister Chloe and she didn't talk about it either.

"Oh, I see. Do your mum and dad argue a lot?"

asked the shopkeeper.

"All the time," Peter sighed.

The shopkeeper pursed his lips. "Hhmm! I think I have just the present you need – for your whole family."

The shopkeeper went around his brightly-coloured counter and disappeared down behind it. Moments later he straightened up, a huge smile on his face and a silver box in his hands.

"These are what you need," he said.

"What are they?" Peter asked doubtfully.

"Christmas crackers," announced the shopkeeper proudly. At the disappointed look on Peter's face, he added, "Ah, but they're not just any crackers. They're magic. Guaranteed to work or your money back."

"How are they magic?" Peter asked suspiciously.

"The magic only works if they're pulled on Christmas Day, when you're all around the table eating dinner," explained the shopkeeper.

"But how do they work?"

"It's hard to explain. You have to see the magic for yourself."

"How much are they?" asked Peter, still doubtful.

Maybe he could buy them and still get the other presents as well.

"I'm afraid they're very expensive because they're magic," said the shopkeeper. "They'll cost you all the money you've got and even then I'm letting you have them cheap."

Peter thought for a moment. Magic crackers. Crackers that would actually stop Mum and Dad from arguing. They were worth the money if they could do that. He took a deep breath.

"All right, I'll take them," he said quickly, before he could change his mind.

Peter handed over his money and the shopkeeper handed over the box of eight crackers. Moments later, Peter was out of the shop and running all the way home. Magic crackers! He couldn't wait for Christmas Day.

"I've been in that kitchen since seven o'clock this morning. I think the least you could do is sit at the table with the rest of your family." Mum's voice dripped with ice.

"I want to watch the end of this film," Dad argued.

"Typical! You're so selfish," Mum snapped.

Peter and Chloe looked at each other and sighed. Mum and Dad were at it again. Christmas Day – and they were still arguing.

"Dad, you and Mum and Chloe can open my present now," Peter said desperately. "The man in the Christmas Shop said they should only be opened when we're all sitting round the table eating dinner."

"Oh, all right then," Dad grumbled.

"Oh, I see. You'll come to the table if Peter asks you to, but not if I ask you," sniffed Mum.

"Peter doesn't nag me every two seconds," Dad said as he sat down at the table.

Chloe shook her head and turned to look out of the window. Peter ran to get the present he'd bought. It was the only one left unopened under the tree. He stood between his mum and dad, putting the present down on the tablecloth. Mum and Dad looked at each other.

"Go on then," Dad prompted.

"You do it," said Mum.

"I'll do it," said Chloe.

She tore off the bright red and yellow wrapping paper.

"It's a box of crackers," she said, surprised.

"Not just any crackers," Peter said eagerly. "They're magic crackers!"

"Who told you that?" Mum smiled.

"The man in the Christmas Shop," Peter replied.

"Well, let's all sit down. Then we can pull them and get on with our dinner," said Dad, adding under his breath, "And maybe then I can get back to my film."

But the moment they all sat down, something peculiar began to happen. A strange feeling settled over the dinner table. A hopeful, expectant feeling – as if, in spite of themselves, everyone was waiting for something terrific, amazing and spectacular to happen all at once. The noise from the telly was just a distant hum at the other end of the room. Light like warm spring sunshine came from every-one smiling at everyone else as they watched Dad place two crackers beside each plate. Chloe held out her cracker to Dad. Peter held his Christmas cracker out to Mum.

"One! Two! Three!" they all shouted.

Bang! Pop! The sound of exploding crackers filled the room. Chloe and Peter got the biggest parts of the crackers. They both peered down into them.

"They're … they're empty!" Chloe exclaimed.

"No! They can't be," frowned Mum.

"See for yourself," said Chloe, handing over her cracker.

Peter couldn't believe it. Empty… When he remembered the smiling, friendly face of the jolly man with the white beard in the Christmas Shop, he just couldn't believe it. That man wouldn't take his money and sell him a box of nothing – Peter was sure he wouldn't. And yet … and yet, his cracker was empty. Just an empty roll covered with some glossy paper and nothing else. No hats. No jokes. No gifts. Nothing.

"Maybe there were just two duff ones in the box," Mum suggested.

Mum and Dad pulled their crackers next. The same thing happened. They were empty. Chloe and Peter pulled crackers five and six at the same time as Mum and Dad pulled crackers seven and eight.

They were all empty.

Peter examined each one, hoping against hope that they'd got it wrong or it was a trick – but it wasn't. Peter looked at Chloe, then Mum and Dad – and burst into tears. He couldn't help it.

"The shopkeeper told me they were magic crackers," Peter sobbed to Mum and Dad. "I only bought them because he said they would make you stop arguing with each other. He promised me they were magic. He promised me…"

Dad stared. Mum's mouth fell open.

"You … you bought them – because of us?" Dad asked, aghast.

Peter sniffed and nodded.

"Never mind, Peter." Chloe put her arm around her younger brother's shoulder. "Besides, nothing would stop Mum and Dad from fighting. Not even a real box of magic crackers." And with that, Chloe burst into tears too.

"Chloe! Peter!" Mum and Dad ran around the

table to hug Peter and Chloe to them. "We had no idea we were quarrelling that much."

"And we had no idea we were upsetting both of you so much," said Dad.

But Peter and Chloe couldn't stop crying.

"I'll tell you what," said Mum. "Let's make our own Christmas crackers. All this food will stay warm in the oven until we've finished."

"Terrific idea." Dad went over to the telly and switched it off. "We'll make the hats first," Dad continued. "Out of newspaper."

Dad and Mum showed Peter and Chloe how to make sailor hats out of newspaper. That took about five minutes. Then they all sat down for dinner. Over dinner, everyone had to tell the worst jokes they knew, like, "How do you make an apple puff? Chase it round the garden!" and "Why did the elephant cross the road? Because it was the chicken's day off!" Dad's joke was "Why did silly Billy stand on a ladder when he was learning to sing? So he could reach the high notes!" And Mum's joke was ancient but she was still proud of it! "How do you make a Swiss Roll? Push him down a hill!" Chloe told a joke that Peter didn't get until Mum explained it. "How do you tell how old a telephone is? Count its rings!" (Mum explained that you could tell the age of a tree by counting the rings through its trunk.) Everyone got Peter's joke. "Why are vampires crazy? Because they're often bats!" And when anyone ran out of jokes, they made them up, which was even funnier!

After dinner when everyone was eating Christmas pudding, Mum grabbed Dad and whispered in his ear. Suddenly they both dashed off upstairs with the empty crackers. Ten minutes later they reappeared with the various ends of each cracker now glued together.

"Cracker time!" said Mum. And she held out a cracker to Chloe.

They both pulled.

"POP!" shouted Mum.

Chloe looked inside the cracker and there was one of Mum's old bangles – the gold and blue one which had always been Chloe's favourite.

"Your turn," said Dad, holding out a cracker to Peter. They both shouted, "BANG!"

136

Peter looked inside the cracker. There was a pig made of lego bricks. At least, that's what Peter thought it was.

"It's not a pig. It's a rocket!" said Dad, indignantly.

Mum started to giggle. "I told you it looked more like a pig, dear," she said.

They "popped" the rest of the crackers. They all had very silly, very tacky, very wonderful presents in them.

"Who needs rotten, mouldy old crackers?" asked Dad. "We can do it all ourselves."

"And they're much better too," Mum agreed. "It's just a shame that Peter got conned out of his money. Where did you say the shop was?"

"Behind the precinct. All the other shops on the same street were boarded up," Peter replied.

"There aren't any shops behind the precinct. The last one closed down over a year ago," Dad frowned.

"There's one still open. It's called the Christmas Shop," said Peter.

Mum and Dad looked at each other. They both shrugged.

"Never mind. I'd say they were the best crackers we've ever had," smiled Mum. "My jaw still aches from laughing at all those terrible jokes."

"Those crackers were … a box of magic," said Dad, giving Mum a cuddle.

Later that night, as Peter lay in bed, he still couldn't quite believe what had happened. Mum and Dad hadn't argued once since the crackers had been pulled. In fact it was the most wonderful day they'd all had in a long, long time. The only cloud was the shopkeeper who'd sold Peter the crackers in the first place. Peter still didn't want to believe that the shopkeeper was a crook who had deliberately diddled him out of his money.

A strange tinkling-clinking came from across the room, followed by a plopping sound. Peter sat up and frowned. What was that? He switched on his bedside light. There it was again – the same strange noise. And it seemed to be coming from his chair over by the window. Over the back of the chair were the jumper and the pair of trousers Peter had worn on Christmas Eve. That strange noise couldn't be coming from them – could it?

Swallowing hard, Peter got up and tiptoed across to the chair.

Tinkle! Clinkle! Plop!

There it was again! Peter took a deep breath, counted to three, then quickly pulled the chair to one side. More money fell out of his trouser pockets and plopped on to the carpet. Peter's eyes goggled! Where had all that money come from? He scooped up the money on the floor, then picked up his trousers and dug into his pockets. There was more money inside them. He counted it all very carefully. It was the exact amount of money he had paid for the Christmas crackers...

Peter sat down on his bed and stared down at the money in his hand. What was going on? He shook his head and looked around the room hoping for some clue. Had Mum and Dad done it? Had they put the money in his pockets to make up for him losing his money in the Christmas Shop? But they didn't know exactly how much he'd paid for the crackers. And now here he was, with the exact same coins in his hand.

Then something else caught his eye. There on

his bedside table, were all the Christmas cards he'd received from his friends. At the front was the card he'd got from his best friend Andy. Peter gasped and stared so hard, his eyes began to ache.

The face on the card...

Peter had seen that face before – in the Christmas Shop. The shopkeeper and Father Christmas were one and the same person... Peter picked up the card and studied it. The shopkeeper was Father Christmas. Peter was sure of it. And that would explain how he'd got his money back. Which meant only one thing...

The Christmas crackers were magic after all.

"Thank you," Peter whispered to the Christmas card.

And he was sure that on the card, the smiling face of Father Christmas winked at him.

Just Like an Angel

Gillian Cross

Gabriel was the youngest in the family, and he wasn't like his brothers. Michael, Richard and Edward were long-legged and cheerful, with blond hair and blue eyes, but Gabriel was small and shy. The others teased him about everything.

Especially angels.

It started when he was four. They were on their way to stay with Grandmother, for the Christmas carol service. As they drove into her village, Gabriel looked out of the car window and saw big, white shapes circling in the sky. They were moving slowly, with the winter sunlight glancing off their wings.

They weren't aeroplanes. Gabriel knew that aeroplanes moved faster, and made a noise. He lifted his hand and pointed.

"Look! Angels!"

Michael and Richard and Edward fell about laughing.

"Hey, Mum! Gabe thinks those are *angels!*"

"Leave him alone," Mrs Jennings said. "They're gliders, Gabriel. Like aeroplanes without engines. They ride on the air currents."

Her voice was kind, but she was laughing too. She couldn't help it. As they drove up the main street of the village, she stopped at the petrol pumps, and told Mr King the garage man, speaking slowly and clearly, so that he could see what she was saying.

"Gabriel thought the gliders were angels."

Gabriel shrank back into the car, waiting for Mr King to laugh. But he didn't. He stroked his long beard, thoughtfully, and smiled into the car.

"Funny you should say that. I often think the same thing, when I'm up in my glider. *Just like being an angel…*"

Suddenly, Gabriel didn't feel stupid any more. He sat up straight, and smiled back at Mr King. And his brothers leaned out of the car windows, calling out in loud, clear voices.

"Have you really got a glider?"

"Will you take us up in it?"

"Please!"

There was no more teasing that day. But Michael and Richard and Edward didn't forget. All the year, they roared with laughter if anyone mentioned angels. And when they were on the way to Grandmother's again, next Christmas, Michael pointed up at the sky.

"Hey, Gabe! After the carol service – when I've sung the solo – we might go up in Mr King's glider."

"*Really?*" Gabriel's eyes glittered, and he bounced up and down in his seat. "Me too?"

"Why don't you ask?" Michael said solemnly. "Look, we're just going past the garage."

Gabriel was so excited that he stuck his head out of the window. "Mr King! Can I go in your glider?"

"What's that?" Mr King came forward, out of his little glass cabin. "Say it again, lad."

But Michael didn't give him a chance. He stuck his head out too. "Gabriel wants a ride in your glider. He thinks he'll turn into an angel."

Mr King didn't laugh, but Gabriel realized that it was just a tease. He went pink and pulled his head back into the car.

The next day, Michael sang the solo at the carol

service, and all the old ladies muttered about what an angel he was. Gabriel shrank down into the pew. It felt just as if they were laughing at him.

That was Michael's last year as an angel. In June, his voice broke, and he couldn't do anything except growl and croak. When Christmas came, it was Richard who sang the solo. And two years after that, Edward had to take over.

It was a tradition in Grandmother's village. The first verse of the first carol had always been sung as a solo, by a child.

> *O come, all ye faithful,*
> *Joyful and triumphant,*
> *O come ye, O come ye*
> *To Bethlehem…*

But there were no children in the choir any more – hardly any children in the village, in fact. So, every year, one of Gabriel's brothers sang instead, with his fair hair gleaming and his blue eyes bright. And all the old men in the congregation smiled, and the old women dabbed at their eyes.

146

And Gabriel sat there wondering how Michael (or Richard or Edward) could be so brave. Singing in front of all those people.

Then, when Gabriel was eight, Edward's voice broke. One day, just before Christmas, he came down to breakfast and started singing, and everyone burst out laughing.

Gabriel laughed too – but not for long. Because Edward grinned at him.

"Looks like you'll be singing the solo this Christmas."

"*Me?*" It came out in a strangled squeak.

"You!" Michael and Richard and Edward yelled. And they laughed even more. They thought he was fussing about nothing.

"It's easy," Michael said. "You just need a bit of practice."

They stood Gabriel on a chair and Richard started humming, pretending to be the organ. "Come on, now. Sing. *O come all ye faithful…*"

Gabriel tried. But the more he tried, the less noise he could make. When he looked round at the three of them, all staring, he felt as if he were choking to death. The only sound that would come out of his mouth was a strangled squeak.

"*O cme all ye fthfl…*"

The others burst out laughing and he jumped off the chair and ran upstairs. And after that, when anyone suggested practising, he looked away and mumbled that he'd done enough practising.

"Dne nff pracsing."

Everyone believed him. And they were sure he would be all right. Why shouldn't he be? Singing was easy. Nobody knew how scared he was.

The nearer they got to Christmas, the worse it grew. When they were actually in the car, on the way to Grandmother's, he was so scared that he thought he was going to faint. He couldn't smile, even though his brothers tried all the old jokes.

"Look, Gabe. Angels up in the sky!"

"Mr King's going to give us a ride in one of those gliders."

"After you've sung your solo."

Gabriel turned away and stared out of the window. He knew he was running out of time. When they arrived at Grandmother's, he had to go straight to bed. And the next day it was the carol service.

The moment he opened his eyes, he thought, *I've got to practise. Before it's too late.* Maybe he would be all right if he found a place where no one could hear him.

He walked down to the far end of the garden and hid behind a rhododendron bush. But the moment he opened his mouth, he began to worry that someone would come. And he made the same strangled sounds as before. *O cme all ye fthful...*

He tried locking himself in the bathroom and turning on all the taps. But was the noise really loud enough to drown out his voice? Before he could make up his mind, Grandmother banged on the door, to ask him why he was wasting all that water.

He tried putting his head under the bedclothes, with all the pillows heaped on top. But that just made him suffocate, so that he gasped and panted. *O-ho c-h-me all ye f-h-thf-h-l...*

And then it was lunchtime. And he'd just picked up his knife and fork when Grandmother said, "All ready for the rehearsal then, Gabriel?"

"Rehearsal?" Gabriel stared.

Michael grinned. "Gabriel doesn't need a rehearsal."

"Nonsense!" Grandmother said briskly. "You all went to the rehearsal. That's why you sang so well. Gabriel must rehearse too. I'll take him down to church as soon as we've washed up."

Gabriel had forgotten about the rehearsal. He'd hardly noticed last year, when Edward slipped off to church in the afternoon. But he remembered now, and he knew he couldn't do it.

He couldn't walk into the church with Grandmother, and stand in front of all those men and women in the choir and sing *O cme all ye fthfl…* He couldn't.

He would have to run away.

He didn't manage to eat much lunch, but everyone just smiled and said he was excited. Then they all went off to the kitchen to wash up in Double Quick Time. Grandmother liked everything done in Double Quick Time. Gabriel waited until they were laughing and talking and teasing each other. Then he opened the front door and slipped out.

There were only two ways to go – left and right. The road to the left went up to the church, so he turned the other way, automatically. He went downhill, towards the garage, running as fast as he could, to get out of sight before anyone saw him.

He ran too fast. As he passed the garage, he caught his foot on a loose stone and went tumbling over, scraping his knees along the ground and banging his head on the Tarmac.

For a moment he just lay there, thinking that things were as bad as they could possibly be. Then he remembered that they would be even worse if anyone caught him, because he'd have to go to the rehearsal. He groaned and started dragging himself up.

But he was too late. Mr King had seen him fall over. He came out of the little glass office behind the petrol pumps and inspected Gabriel's knees.

"Nasty fall," he said calmly. "Come in and have a barley sugar."

For a moment, Gabriel thought of running away. Then he realized that Mr King might run after him. He followed him into the glass cabin, limping a bit.

Mr King unhooked a bag of barley sugars from the display, opened it and gave one to Gabriel. Then he said, "What are you doing down here this afternoon? I thought you'd be up at the church. Rehearsing."

That was the last straw. Before he could stop himself, Gabriel burst into tears.

Mr King pulled a handkerchief out of his pocket and unfolded it. He watched Gabriel wipe his eyes and then said, "What's up?"

"Gt t sng n the crl svice," mumbled Gabriel, with his face in his hands. "Nd m scared—"

"No use talking like that," Mr King said. "You know I can't hear. Take your hands away from your mouth and let me lip-read."

Gabriel had forgotten Mr King was deaf. Dropping his hands, he made himself speak clearly. He was concentrating so hard on making the shapes of the words with his lips, that he didn't worry about what he was saying.

"I've got to sing the solo at the carol service. And I'm scared."

Mr King nodded. "Not surprised. There's only one way to get over that. Practice."

Gabriel hung his head. "Bt—" Then he remembered about Mr King's deafness, and he started again. "But if I practise, the others laugh at me."

"So you can't sing? In case they laugh?"

Gabriel nodded.

Mr King gave him another barley sugar and walked up and down for a bit. Then he stopped and looked at Gabriel.

"Want to come up in a glider?"

"Me?" Gabriel was so amazed that he didn't mumble at all. Mr King had never offered any of the others a flight. Even though they'd begged him, for years and years. "Just me?"

"Just you," Mr King said. "Come on."

They walked out of the cabin and he locked it behind them. Then he turned the big sign at the front of the forecourt, so that it said CLOSED instead of OPEN.

"We've just got time before it's too dark. If we hurry."

They climbed into his Land Rover and it started with a judder and bounced down the hill towards Mr King's house. When they got there, Mr King put on the brake, very noisily, and said something.

Gabriel couldn't hear at first, because of the engine. Then he remembered about lip-reading and he saw what Mr King was saying. *Wait there while I fetch my brothers.*

There were two brothers. They both had beards, but one was fat and one was thin. They smiled as they climbed into the back of the Land Rover. With a crash of gears, Mr King drove out of the village and up to the glider field.

Gabriel had been to the field dozens of times. Whenever they came to the village, his brothers walked up there and stared longingly at the hangar where Mr King kept his red and white glider. If he was there, Mr King would smile and wave to them, but he never asked them into the field.

This time, he drove straight in and round the track at the edge of the field.

"Stay in the Land Rover," he said to Gabriel.

Gabriel knew what was going to happen, because he'd seen it before. He watched Mr King's brothers open the hangar and wheel out the glider. He watched Mr King prepare the winch, and unwind the long cable that would pull the glider into the air.

The brothers settled the glider at the far end of the field and left it there, with the sun gleaming on its red and white paint. Then they came back up to the hangar. The fat brother found a helmet.

"Scared?" he said, as he adjusted the straps round Gabriel's chin.

"No." Gabriel didn't see how anyone could be scared about going up in a glider. How could you be afraid of something wonderful?

Climbing into the cockpit, he settled himself in the front seat, with Mr King behind him. His heart was thudding against his ribs, but he knew he wasn't scared. He was excited.

The thin brother held on to the glider's wing and the fat one went down the field, to start the winch. Suddenly, the glider was racing forward, pulled by the cable. The thin brother ran along beside, holding it level.

"Here we go!" said Mr King.

And the glider took off.

It went up like a bird. Like an arrow shot from a

bow. Rising into the air like something speeding up a steep, steep hill. Gabriel felt himself being pushed against the back of his seat. Up and up and up…

And then they stopped climbing.

"Look over the side," Mr King's voice said, from behind.

Gabriel turned his head and saw the winch cable falling away as the glider levelled out. The cable had done its work and pulled them up, just as the string pulls a kite. Now they were in the sky, floating free. Riding the currents of the air.

It was very quiet. The only sounds Gabriel could hear were the creak of the wooden wings and the hiss of air round his head. He was sitting high in the sky, with nothing to shut him in.

Far below, he could see the village. The church where the choir was singing. The cars racing round the bypass. A train in the distance. They were all too far away to hear.

For a few minutes, the glider circled slowly, and Gabriel stared round. He was amazed how clearly he could see everything, even though it was such a long way down. It was like looking at the whole world.

"Beautiful, isn't it?" Mr King said.

Gabriel nodded. There was no way of saying how beautiful it was.

Mr King gave a small, soft chuckle. "Always makes me want to sing."

"*Do* you sing?" Gabriel said. "Up here on your own?"

There was another chuckle. "No use talking. I can't lip-read from here. Can't hear a thing you're saying."

For a second, Gabriel felt stupid.

And then he understood what Mr King was telling him. They were up there on their own, just the two of them. And Mr King was deaf. *So no one could possibly hear any singing. No one in the whole world!*

But – wasn't it ridiculous? Singing in a glider?

Gabriel looked over the side, at the grey church spire, and the glittering line of the brook, and the big hills stretching away into the distance. The lovely, sunlit world. No, singing wasn't ridiculous. It was the only sensible thing to do.

He opened his mouth.

* * *

O come all ye faithful,
Joyful and triumphant…

It felt wonderful. Like yelling hurrah. Like blowing a fanfare on a trumpet.

Like being an angel.

The white wings of the glider gleamed in the winter sunshine. There was a small green car driving round the bypass. Maybe there was a little boy inside. Looking up at the glider and thinking it was an angel. Gabriel took a deep breath and sang as loudly and sweetly as he could.

O come let us adore him,
O come let us adore him,
O come let us adore him,
Christ the Lord!

He was still singing as the glider circled lower over the field. He didn't even realize they were landing, until they bumped lightly on to the grass, and Mr King's brothers came running forward to help him out of his seat.

"That was a nice bit of singing," said the thin brother.

"Look forward to hearing you in church," said the fat brother.

Gabriel went pink and hung his head. "Bt tht's diffrnt."

Mr King tapped his shoulder. "What did you say?"

Gabriel felt silly, but he turned round and spoke clearly. "I said that's different. Singing in church."

"Don't see why," Mr King said. "Shut your eyes, and you can be anywhere you like."

The brothers both nodded, and Gabriel frowned. What did they mean?

"Time to go home," Mr King said. "I'll take you up. These two will put the glider away. Hop in the Land Rover, lad."

As Gabriel climbed in, he suddenly wondered what he was going to say when he got back to Grandmother's house. She would be furious with him. How could he explain why he'd run away?

He didn't have to explain anything. When they reached the house, Mr King went in on his own, leaving Gabriel to wait in the Land Rover. When he came out again, Grandmother was with him. She was smiling.

"You've missed the rehearsal, but it sounds as though you don't need one. Mr King tells me you're a wonderful singer."

"But—" *But Mr King can't hear…*

Grandmother didn't give Gabriel time to say it. She caught hold of his arm. "Hurry up, or we'll be late for the service."

Michael came bounding out of the house in his best clothes. "Gabriel can't go to church like that. He's wearing jeans."

"Don't be silly," Grandmother said. "And anyway, no one will see when he's got the choir robes on. Come along, Gabriel."

She hustled him down the path, with the rest of the family scurrying behind. Michael ran to catch up, whispering in Gabriel's ear.

"Where have you been?"

"In a glider," Gabriel said.

"Oh, ha ha!" Michael pulled a face. "Stop teasing."

Teasing? "Mr King took me up."

Richard jogged up. "Don't be silly. The garage is

open on Friday afternoons. Mr King must have been there."

Gabriel couldn't answer, because they'd reached the church, and Grandmother was chivvying him round to the vestry. She buttoned him into a long blue cassock and slipped a white surplice over his head. Then she nodded approvingly.

"You look very nice. Even better than your brothers."

Gabriel didn't care how he looked. As she pushed him into line with the rest of the choir, he was shaking. And when they walked into church, he nearly fainted. All the front pews were full. People were going to *hear* him. He couldn't sing. He *couldn't*.

The organist began the introduction to the first carol. Gabriel felt his throat go dry. He knew he wouldn't be able to make any sound except a squeak. He knew it. But there was no escape.

He opened his mouth.

And then, at the last moment, he saw Mr King, sitting at the back of the church, looking at him. Slowly and deliberately, Mr King closed his eyes.

Shut your eyes, and you can be anywhere you like.

All at once, Gabriel understood. He closed his own eyes – and he wasn't looking at rows of people any more. He was in the glider, circling like an angel. The sunshine was glittering on the snow-white wings, and the beautiful world was spread out below.

He started to sing, as sweetly as he could.

O come all ye faithful…

He didn't open his eyes until the whole carol was over. When he did, he saw his brothers, sitting in the front pew, staring at him. Wondering whether it could be possibly true about the glider. He almost burst out laughing.

But he didn't laugh. He stared straight ahead, looking solemn and good, and he heard the old ladies whispering to each other.

"Just like an angel…"

I'll do it even better next year, he thought. And he started smiling. He had years and years left before his voice broke. Years and years of being a Christmas angel.